He's A Good Guy Just Not Yours

MARTHA KILBY

MORE EXCELLENT
WAY ENTERPRISES

Publisher:
MEWE, LLC
Lithonia, GA
www.mewellc.com

First Edition
ISBN: 978-0-9988281-3-8

Library of Congress Number: 2017905900

For Worldwide Distribution
Printed in the USA

To the lover of my soul, Jesus Christ. Thank you for loving me beyond what I thought I deserve. My heart's desire is to forever be in love with you.

AUTHOR'S NOTE

This book is a work of fiction. Yes, that means I made it up. Although portions of this novel are inspired from real events, each character in it is fictional. There's a biblical saying that allows us to know that there's nothing new under the sun; so, no I didn't reinvent the wheel on how many young people fall in love ☺. However, I've often heard, if you want to write a good novel, go out and have an adventure. While life's adventures have been rewarding, no reference to any person, living or deceased, is intended or should be inferred. 'Preciate it! Happy Reading!

Momma 3,
VeVa! Thank you for
ALL your support! Our
connection means the
world to me. And I
appreciate you!
♡ Malla

ACKNOWLEDGEMENTS

I am grateful for the partners and friends of The Harvest Tabernacle Church in Lithonia, Georgia, for supporting me in this endeavor.

I would like to thank my spiritual father and life coach, Apostle Travis C. Jennings for your consistency in pushing me into greater every time I hear you speak. You are the real M.V.P. for this dream being birth into a reality.

I would like to thank my spiritual mother and mentor, Pastor Stephanie L. Jennings for speaking the vision God had for my life. Your encouragement throughout this entire project will forever be priceless.

I would like to thank Dr. Kemberly McKenzie for the countless hours spent with me to complete this project. You are an angel in disguise and I am truly grateful for you.

I would like to thank Shenee' Henry of Paper Trail, LLC, for rescuing me when this project came overwhelming in the last hour. I will never forget your selfless act of kindness towards me and the publication of this assignment.

Lastly, I would like to thank my support system. Everyone that encouraged me, sowed into this project with money or time, continued to ask me how the book was coming along, always listened when I read bits and pieces aloud, and just for being God sent. You all know who you are. Thank you! Thank you! Thank you!

CHAPTER I

The crisp fall air blew across Alexandria's face as she sat in the passenger seat of her brother's Honda Accord. The nighttime was drawing near, and they were on their way to choir rehearsal at their family church. Alexandria had four siblings, two sisters, and her two brothers. They were all four years apart. However, the sibling closest to her was her brother, Steven, who was nearest to her in age. She and her brother used their time in the car together to either talk about life, listen to music or simply sang at the top of their lungs to the hit songs on the radio.

Alexandria was a sophomore in high school, honor roll student and a member of the varsity cheerleading and track teams. This particular day, Alexandria sat quietly as the music blasted loudly from the speakers of the car. She stuck her hand out of the window and let the wind blow in between her fingers; she found the vibration relaxing. A few seconds later, her phone went off. As she read the incoming text, her thumbs quickly stroked the keys to respond to the incoming message from a guy she liked at school.

LANDON:	Thinking of you... What are you doing?
ALEX:	On my way to rehearsal...What are your thoughts telling you about me? ☺
LANDON:	Lol. That you should call me...
ALEX:	I'm in the car with my brother, so I will call you when I'm free ☺

Alexandria smiled, looking down at her cell phone as she felt her pulse began to race. She began to think about how soon she would be able to call him. Steven interrupted her thoughts with a brotherly question.

"Who was that?" She quickly responded, "Oh, just that guy I was telling you about from my English class."

"Is this the new kid at school that you said got kicked off the football team already?" he asked. He looked puzzled because she still seemed interested.

"Ummmm. Yea," she said laughing.

"Well, what happened to the basketball player that you were trying to work things out with?"

She took a deep breath and said, "You mean Justin? Ummm, I just don't want to go back and forth or fight for something if he doesn't really believe that we should be together, you know? I mean, Justin is sweet and everything, but this guy is different."

It had only been a couple of weeks since Justin broke things off with Alexandria, and she was already entertaining a new love interest. Justin was Alexandria's tenth boyfriend in a four-year time span. They met during freshman year in History class; however, they were only friends initially. At the time, Alexandria wasn't at all preoccupied with having a boyfriend. She was really focused on just getting adjusted to high school, staying above average in her classes and of course, doing well in competitive cheerleading and track. It wasn't until her sophomore year that they decided that they wanted to take their friendship to the next level.

She had considered Justin, a really respectable guy with the only downside coming from the fact that he was very timid. On the other hand, she was very jovial with an outgoing personality. Justin was indeed a lot like the other guys she dated in the past, but when he heard that Alexandria liked someone else, he broke up with her. No questions were asked and no reasons were given for his decision to call it quits with her. He simply told her it wasn't going to work out. Though Alexandria was hurt, she didn't bother to ask him why.

Moments later, her brother pulled into a gas station. A grin ran across Alexandria's face as she realized this would probably be the only moment that she would be able to call her new crush, Landon. As Steven got out of the car, she quickly browsed through her contacts to find his number.

Ring! Ring! Ring!

"Hey Alex, you called?" Landon said. His tone was anxious yet excited.

"Yea. I know you weren't expecting me to call right now – so consider yourself lucky!" she said.

Alexandria was excited to be on the phone, but she aimed to hide it from him. Landon laughed at her comment, as he thought to himself how he'd never met a girl that was so confident and quick witted.

"Oh really?" he laughed. "I thought you were with your brother, Steven?"

"I am. But he's pumping gas now so I thought I would let you hear my voice."

Landon was quiet. Smiling at the other end, he said, "Girl, you know I like the fact that you're so silly."

Alexandria felt butterflies in her stomach as she replayed Landon's words through her mind.

She quickly asked, "Landon, are you admitting you like me?"

Landon had one mission when he asked for Alexandria's number, and that was to make her his girlfriend. Rumors were going around school when she was still dating Justin that Alexandria told one of her best friends that she thought Landon was cute. At that point, he had a gut feeling that Alexandria liked him as well, but he wasn't sure if she would think it was too soon to become an item. She just got out of a relationship, and they barely knew one another.

Still, he thought she was pleasant and good looking. He'd told himself: *If I tell her I like her and ask her to be my girlfriend, it won't hurt anything. I mean, we have already hung out a couple of times.*

Then Landon replied softly, "Girl, you know I like you! The real question is do you like me?"

Alexandria smiled, pressed her back deeper into the car seat and giggled. "Why does that matter?" she asked.

Landon loved talking to Alexandria and would usually play the question game with her, but he really wanted her to be his girlfriend. He laughed out loud.

"Alex, you're funny. It matters because if you did like me, I'd want you to be my girl."

Alexandria thought, *he wants me to be his girl?!* No guy had ever talked to her like that. Landon was strong and straight forward. She liked it.

"Of course I like you," she said quietly. A comfortable silence interrupted their conversation.

"Well, would you be my girlfriend?" Landon finally blurted out.

Without any hesitation, Alexandria responded, "Look, I just got out of a relationship, and I'm not looking for someone to just kick it with. I need some kind of commitment."

She was to be applauded at knowing what she wanted. She didn't know how Landon would feel about the long-term clause in the agreement. However, all Alexandria knew was that after being in ten relationships within the space of four years, and only one out of the ten lasting a year and a half, she was honestly tired of being so unconstrained.

Alexandria's parents were married, and she lived in a stable environment. However, Landon grew up in a divorced home. His parents divorced when he was eight. Although he chose to stay with his mom, he deeply desired a relationship with his father. Landon felt like the needed to be there for his mom after his father left. His mom had just recently downsized from the house he grew up in. But all Landon and his brother really wanted was for their parents to get back together. Landon desired a stable relationship too, and he saw Alexandria as someone that he could be stable with if she wanted it as well.

"That's exactly what I want," Landon responded.

Alexandria thought *this is too good to be true.* She further asked him, "Are you sure?"

"I am," Landon responded.

She asked again, "Are you sure?"

Landon chuckled and said, "Yes!"

For a final time, she inquired, "Landon, are you sure that you're sure?"

He responded, "Alex, I promise you. I'm sure."

With a smile on her face, butterflies in her stomach and a peace of mind, she finally said, "Ok then, I will be your happily ever after."

Landon was relieved to hear her response. She was officially his girlfriend, and he couldn't wait to tell his friends.

"Hey my brother is walking back to the car so, I have to go. Text me!" she said. She hung up the phone in a hurry.

Alexandria was so excited; she couldn't wait to tell her brother about what just happened. As they were pulling out of the gas station, she blurted out with excitement, "So Landon, the new guy I was telling you about, just asked me to be his GIRLFRIEND!!!"

Steven looked over at her and said, "So, when do I get to meet him?"

"Soon," she responded.

"Ok, Alex. Remember nothing changes. You always get overly excited, but don't forget what I told you." He scolded her.

"I won't. Nothing changes, and you will meet him! Trust me, I don't want to be in another counseling session!" she chuckled.

***

The relationship was blossoming, and Landon and Alexandria were the hot new couple at school. They went everywhere and did everything together.

"Where are you?" Alexandria asked Landon.

"I'm walking up."

"Ok. I'm coming out."

Alexandria hung up the phone, ran out of her aunt's house and threw her arms around Landon's neck, giving him a big hug. It was convenient that her aunt, Liz, lived in the same neighborhood as Landon. He squeezed her back and gave her a kiss on her forehead. It had been two months, and the winter was drawing nearer. A strong gust of wind blew and she threw her face into his chest, wrapping her arms around his waist as they started towards the front door.

"You smell really good," she said.

"You like it? My pops got it for me," he replied.

"Yea. So how long can you stay tonight?" she asked.

"I told my momma we were just gonna hang out and watch a movie, so I guess until she calls."

She opened the door to her aunt's house and walked in while Landon followed behind her. As he closed the door, the temperature inside grew much warmer.

"It feels good in here," he said.

"I know, cozy right?" she said, tugging on the sides of Landon's jacket as she pulled him closer to give him a hug.

As they walked through the foyer to the family room, Alexandria said to Landon, "You can make yourself comfortable in here. I'm gonna run into the kitchen real quick. Do you want anything to drink?"

"Nah. I'm good."

Alexandria left the room and Landon made his way over to the couch. He began to look at the photos that were hung up of Alexandria's family, and he admired how close her family was. A few minutes later, Alexandria returned from the kitchen with a bowl of popcorn and a couple of drinks on a food tray. Landon gazed in her direction as she was making her way to the coffee table and asked. "Where's your aunt?"

"Oh. She's working late at the salon tonight. So, we're here alone."

"Really?"

Alexandria sat the tray down and then started to back away from the couch and replied jokingly. "Yes, really. So, you make sure you be on your best behavior." As she continued to move backward.

Landon smiled. "Why are you standing so far away?" Holding out his hand in her direction, he mouthed *come here*.

Alexandria turned around to walk in the opposite direction of where he wanted her. "Well, before I sit down, what movie do you want to watch? I'm giving you a chance to pick now because when I put in '*The Notebook*' you have to promise to pay attention! It's my favorite movie of all time – that and '*Love and Basketball*.'"

Landon laughed. "Ha ha ha. Very funny."

There was silence as Alexandria sat on the floor and skimmed through the DVDs in the case.

"Alex?"

"Yea?"

"I know that we've talked about this so, please don't get mad or anything, but what exactly happened that night with Nathan, Will, and Slim?"

"What do you mean? I told you already." she shot back in a surprising angry tone.

"Nah. I mean, you said that what I heard was true. But you never told me from your side what really happened."

"What's there to tell? It is what it is... Honestly, Landon, I don't mind being open with you. I just feel it's a little unfair that you can bring up my past, and I don't know anything about yours. And please don't use that lame excuse that you have to go to school with them."

"Baby com'on. You know that if there's anything you want to know about my past I'd tell you."

Alexandria dreaded talking about her past relationships. Nathan, Will and Slim were all football players. Although she never dated Slim, she did date Will for a short time in middle school. Nath, however, was her middle school sweetheart. She knew that Landon just wanted to understand the situation better, but she just wanted to leave the past where it belonged - in the past. Ever since middle school, it seemed as though she was always with a new guy, and before they started dating, Landon asked her straight out if she had ever hooked up with Nathan, Will, and Slim. It was an old rumor that a couple of people at school told him about. Alexandria told him without hesitation that she did. He found her honesty very attractive, and it kind of made him want to be with her even more. He felt as though she didn't allow it to shape who she was. However, there was always an uneasy feeling he got when he passed by any of the guys in the hallway at school. He just felt he needed a little more information to ease his mind.

"Whatever," Alexandria said, annoyed. She stayed seated on the floor near the DVD stand, facing the direction of where Landon was sitting on the couch. "Look, this is the last time I want to talk about this." She paused, then said, "Nathan and I were together for about a year and a half. We never fooled around while we were together. Plus, my brother would have killed me! We just hung out. We chilled at the movies, watched football games and just talked a lot on the phone."

"Why did you break up then?" Landon asked.

"I broke things off with him towards the middle of eighth grade year because he started pressuring me to have sex. I was just very uncomfortable with the idea, and it was starting to become overbearing, you know? I would let him finger me, and we would make out, but that was it. After we'd broken up a couple of weeks later, I started dating Sean."

"Sean. The one that plays basketball?" Landon asked.

"Yea, him. We were only together for a couple of weeks, and nothing physical happened between us. After Sean and I broke up, one night at a party, I just fell into the heat of the moment. Honestly, I was just pissed off at Sean and everything else that was going on. At first Slim, Will, Nathan and I were all just talking about school in the kitchen and then one thing led to another... I made out with Will and then Slim, and I let them fool around with me below the belt."

"You let them mess around with you at the same time in the kitchen?" Landon asked, bothered.

Landon really liked Alexandria. He had not envisioned her to be the type of girl to conduct herself in such whorish way. He was upset at the situation because he didn't understand what would make a girl that seemed so confident and sure of herself, do something so stupid.

With a trembling voice and shaky hands, Alexandria asked. "Are you going to make me feel bad about it or listen for your answers? Cause, I really don't have to tell you anything!"

Landon got up and walked over to where she was sitting on the floor. Directly sitting in front of her; he gently grabbed her hands, and looked her in the eyes.

"Sorry for interrupting – I know you don't have to tell me what happened. And I don't want you to be mad at me for asking."

Alexandria looked back in relief that he hadn't walked out. She sighed and said. "No...I want to tell you if it will make you feel better about the situation. But I do already feel bad enough about it as it is."

"I feel you – Let's just watch the movie. We haven't had a fight before and I don't want to start now."

"But I want to finish telling you. I just want this part of our relationship to be over."

"Are you sure?" Landon asked.

"Yes."

Alexandria wanted to tell him, but it wasn't easy because she wasn't confident that it wouldn't change things between them. She was a virgin, and even when they were friends, she always stressed that she would remain a virgin until she got married. She didn't want what happened in the past to dictate what should happen in the relationship they currently had. Landon, on the other hand, wasn't a virgin; however, it never bothered Alexandria much because she never wanted to be with someone that was inexperienced. She wondered every now and then how he could have already had sex with three girls since he was only a sophomore in high school, but she never gave in to it. Maybe it did help that she never knew them.

Alexandria let go of his hands, stood up and began to pace the floor slowly as she gently scratched her forehead. Landon sat looking at her.

Finally, she took a deep breath, turned to him and spoke up. "Will and Slim both made out with me and fingered me. First Will and then Slim. Unfortunately, we were all in the kitchen at the same time. Then after that, Nathan grabbed my hand and led me into a bedroom for what I'm guessing would be more privacy, but Slim followed us. Why?...I guess I will never know... Then Nathan pulled me closer to him and just started kissing me out of nowhere. I was shocked because we weren't even together anymore, and he was with someone else. But in the middle of us kissing, he stopped and asked me if I WOULD GO DOWN ON HIM."

Alexandria paused. Landon, still seated on the floor, was now looking down at the carpet. He could hear the anger in her voice, and he didn't want to see her cry - he wasn't *prepared* to see her like this. Alexandria took a deep breath, gathered her emotions and continued.

"And so I did... I guess I still liked him, you know?" She waited for Landon to say something. She needed him to say anything.

"While Slim was there too?" Landon asked softly finally looking back in her direction.

"Yea... he was there. I had no idea what I was supposed to do, you know? I had never done anything like that before. Then while this was going on, Nathan asked Slim if he had a condom and he said no. I stopped as soon as he said no. I got up, left the party, and I called my brother to pick me up. I just kept walking in the direction of home until I saw my brother's car."

Alexandria began to conjure the feeling she had felt when she left the party, and her eyes started to tear up.

"What did your brother say? Landon asked.

"Nothing. I believe my brother was scared to ask. I just shut down for a while." Alexandria replied. "People whispered at school, but I never heard what they were saying."

"Did you tell anyone? Any of your friends?"

"Nope. I didn't tell any of my friends, and they didn't ask. The only person I ever told was my family's counselor. My mom ended up making me talk to him the summer after eighth grade ended."

Landon got up, walked over to Alexandria and gave her a hug. They stood there hugging in the moment. Alexandria felt a load lifted off of her chest, and Landon felt closer to her than before. They walked over to the couch, cuddled up and began to watch TV. After a few hours, Landon's mom finally called to tell him it was time for him to come home. They said their goodnights and went their separate ways. Everything seemed better than normal; the space that was holding baggage before was now free. Alexandria knew in her heart that if they actually had overcome that hurdle, they would only get stronger.

CHAPTER 2

The next morning, Alexandria went for a run with Steven. They were conditioning together to help her prepare for the upcoming track season. After they came to a stopping point, Alexandria was out of breath. She paced back and forth, and finally, her heart rate slowed down enough for her to talk.

"Wow, that hill gets me every time!" she told him.

"You have to remember to pace yourself!" he scolded her.

"I know. I know," she said.

"If you want to be the best, you don't only have to train like them - you have to think like them too."

"I know."

"Speaking of thinking like the best, how are your grades?" he asked.

"They are ok. I'm still having trouble in Chemistry. I really hate that class."

"I hated it too, but colleges don't care about that. Just make sure you are getting all of your homework done. No zeros, Alex - every point counts!"

"I have been. We've also been able to do group work, so it helps."

"That's good. What about cheerleading? Are you ready for the state competition?"

"I really am. I'm just nervous because I've never competed at that level before."

"You will be fine. Remember what I told you. You qualified and made the same team as everyone else, so you have what it takes to compete with them."

"Yea, and thanks to you, I told one of the senior girls that, and she nearly ripped my head off!" she giggled.

Steven laughed at her. "I told you about that mouth of yours. Not everyone wants or needs to hear every thought that you have."

"Yea, she was pretty upset, but things are okay now." She smiled, assuring him.

"How are things with Landon? Mom tells me you all have been spending a lot of time together."

"Things are great! He's a really good guy! You know he's …"

Steven cut her off. "Yes, I know. He's different." He interrupted her sarcastically. "Just remember that nothing changes, Alex. And I know you hear me tell you this over and over again, but don't forget that."

"You know I actually ended up telling him that I went through counseling?"

"Really? What did he say?" he asked surprised. Alexandria did not tell anyone about what went on in her counseling sessions.

"Well, I just told him about one of the incidents that happened back in middle school. And he was asking me if I told anyone about it besides him, and I told him no, only my family's counselor."

"Don't you think it's kind of soon to talk to him about intimate and personal details of your life? That was a pretty intense time for you." Her brother asked in a concerned tone.

"I didn't tell him everything. I only told him what he asked because he has to go to school with some of the guys, and you know how people are, they talk."

"Well, just be careful and use your brain!" Steven looked at his sister and smiled.

After Alexandria and her brother had finished training that morning, she decided to visit her best friend, Whitley, later that afternoon. Whitley was a junior, and they met during Alexandria's freshman year. They both ran varsity track together and lived in the same subdivision. They had actually gone to the same middle school too but just never really talked. Whitley played on the varsity basketball team and was dating one of the starting men's varsity basketball players.

Alexandria found it easier to keep her friendship with Whitley because she was in a serious relationship just like her. It seemed like the friendships of everyone else she had connected with before entering high school, had died down since she started dating Landon. She didn't really mind it because she believed it was part of growing up. However, Whitley was the person she could talk to whenever she couldn't really talk to Steven about girl stuff. When Alexandria's brother dropped her off at Whitley's house, she walked around to the side entrance through the garage into the kitchen. There she ran into Whitley's mom who was heading out.

"Hi, Mrs. Adams!"

"Well, Hello Alex! I haven't seen you around here in a while. How are you?"

"Everything's great! Cheerleading season is about done, and I've started training for track."

"That's wonderful news! I'm sure you ladies will win region again this year!"

"Yes, ma'am! That's the plan and STATE as well!"

"That's the spirit! I'm glad everything is going so well with you. I'm just heading out to run a couple of errands; but, Whit is down in the basement."

"Ok. Maybe I will see you later on when you get back."

"You're more than welcome to stay for dinner if you'd like."

"Thanks for the invite. I might just take you up on the offer."

Alexandria left the room and headed for the basement where she found Whitley sitting on the couch watching MTV music videos.

"Whit. You're addicted!" She yelled at her friend.

"Well. I heard crack is whack sooooo, yea," Whitley joked back.

Whitley reached for the remote to turn the TV down, and Alexandria plopped down beside her on the couch.

"How was training with your brother?"

"Is that really a question?"

"I guess not. But next time you go, let me know because I definitely don't mind the extra help."

"You say that now and then when I call you..."

"I'm serious," Whitley giggled.

"I'm sure. Anyways what have you been doing besides watching TV all day?"

"Oh, cut the crap Alex and just get to the point!"

Alexandria laughed hysterically at her friend then said. "And this is why we will forever be friends! Sooooo, how was your date night with Randy," she inquired with a girly giggle.

"It was actually really good! Um, we went to a movie and then we had dinner at the Avenue."

"Sounds boring."

"Shut up! Things are very sketchy right now because my parents are always on my back!!"

"So, what does that have to do with Randy?"

"My dad thinks that things are getting too serious between us. And you know the last time I snuck him over here we almost got caught! I just feel like it's becoming too much."

"You sound like you are ready to call it quits!"

"I don't know. I love him, but there are just some things that we would need to change, you know?"

"I guess," Alexandria said puzzled.

Alexandria didn't really understand why Whitley gave Randy such a hard time. They were like the perfect couple and had been together for almost 2 years. Alexandria looked up to Whitley like a big sister; however, Randy was presently pressing Whitley to take their relationship to a more intimate level. Whitley's parents were leaders in the community, not to mention devoted Christians, and image was everything. Whitley loved Randy, but she knew that her dad was right. The night she snuck Randy over could have very well ruined her vow that she made to her parents and God about waiting until marriage to have sex. When her dad almost caught him over at their house, she knew it was time to slow things down.

Then Whitley said, "How's Landon? You guys are just the cutest - couple - EVER! Everyone at school talks about it."

"Everything is good! You know he's different. He's not like the guys from around here. He really is a good guy."

"Yes! Yes! Please remind me!"

Alexandria rolled her eyes and gave Whitley an annoyed look and continued. "The odd part is that my parents actually like him! I mean, I'm not too sure about my dad, but my mom does."

"What about Steven?"

"He's cool too. I mean, you know he has this plan for my life so of course, he would prefer me to be with the star football player!" Alexandria laughed.

Whitley giggled. "Your brother is so funny! He's probably hoping it doesn't last!!"

"I know, right?!"

Smiling at her friend, Whitley asked. "Didn't you guys hang out last night?"

"We did! We kinda had our first argument last night too, but everything ended on a good note."

"Really? I'm shocked! Over what?"

"Some people told him about the incident with Nathan, Will, and Slim."

"I thought you said you already talked to him about it before you started dating?"

"We did. But now he wanted more details," Alexandria said getting annoyed.

"Oh. Well, things are good now, right?"

"Yup. We just cuddled and watched TV. It was perfect!"

"And you called my night boring?" Whitley shot back.

They both laughed. Alexandria and Whitley hung out for the remainder of the afternoon, and she ended up staying for dinner.

Alexandria had a really good support system setup. She had an open relationship with her mother and brother. Although she wasn't as close to her other siblings, her family was very close. All of her friends generally tended to watch out for her. No one had to know everything about her; they just wanted the best for her.

***

A couple of months went by and the school year was coming to an end. Alexandria was about to successfully complete her sophomore year of high school, and things with Landon were going really good. She was sitting in her Geometry class when the dismissal bell rung, and after she had gathered her books, she began to walk towards to classroom door. Standing there waiting for her was Landon.

They always met at her locker, but for some reason today he was at her class.

With a surprised look on her face, she asked, "Missed me that much that you had to stalk me in class, huh?" She giggled as he leaned in and kissed her on the forehead.

"Actually, I never left," he joked.

Alexandria looked at him. "You would be the sweetest guy ever if only you told truths." She laughed. He grabbed her books from her and reached for her hand.

They held hands as they walked down the hall towards her locker. As they got closer, Landon said. "You always beat me to the locker, but I just have to see your face when you open it today."

Then she stopped walking and looked at him inquisitively.

"What did you put in my locker?"

He smiled and looked at her, "The mystery..."

"Landon, if I open this locker and there are flowers you do know you are carrying them the remainder of the day!?" she laughed.

For Valentine's Day, Landon emptied out Alexandria's locker and put two dozen roses in it. She walked around the entire day with roses, a stuffed teddy bear, and balloons. Landon was the type of guy who was publicly affectionate; however, Alexandria preferred private displays of affection. She didn't mind holding hands or a kiss here and there, but constant affection embarrassed her a bit. She and Landon talked about it, but it was just his love language, and everyone else thought it was sweet.

"Quit whining and open the locker," he said as he propped his back up against the locker next to hers. As Alexandria began to open her locker, her heart rate began to speed up because she was nervous and hated surprises. Landon was always full of surprises.

When she opened the door, there was a card. It wasn't in an envelope but just sitting there tented on top of her books. The front of the card read, "I PROMISE..." and then once she picked it up the inside read: "TO BE YOURS FOREVER - YOUR ONE-N-ONLY, LANDON." Her heart dropped because behind the card was a jewelry box. She turned, looked at him and smiled.

He said, "Happy 6 months Anniversary - you have to open it!" She was getting teary eyed as she reached for the box and opened it. Inside was a ring with a blue sapphire princess cut. Her hands shook, and the tears in her eyes began to fall down her cheek. No guy had ever done this for her, she thought. As she began to wipe her face, Landon moved closer towards her and whispered in her ear.

"That moment right there, was priceless."

"I didn't know we were celebrating. I didn't get a gift for you," she said.

"I wanted to do this for you."

"I'm shocked! Wh-what does this ring mean?"

"If you decide that you will wear the ring, and I am hoping that you do, then I'll know that you too promise to be mine forever too."

Then he placed her books in her locker, kissed her moist cheek and walked away.

Alexandria stood there, in amazement to take it all in and gather her emotions. Then the warning bell rung and she quickly grabbed her books for the next class, took the ring out of the box and placed the box back in her locker. She positioned the ring on her ring finger with the biggest smile on her face and hurried to her next class. She couldn't wait to tell Whitley.

CHAPTER 3

Once she got home, she ran up the stairs into her parents' bedroom. Alexandria's mom stayed at home and did a lot of volunteer work for their church.

"Mom!" she yelled, but there was no answer. "Mom! Where are you?" Still no answer.

Alexandria ran down the stairs and headed towards the kitchen. "MOM!"

"What is it?" her mom said as she was coming up the stairs from the basement.

"Guess what happened to me today?"

Her mom looked at her with a blank look. "You found out that you're really adopted?" her mom joked.

"That's not funny. Although, that could very well be true," she joked back.

Alexandria and her mom had an unusually good relationship. She could pretty much talk to her mom about anything and the things that she didn't talk to her mom about her mom somehow already knew. Alexandria always felt that her mom was pretty strict on her. All her siblings felt that since she was the youngest of five, their mom was too lenient with Alexandria.

"So, tell me, what happened?" Her mom said as she made her way to the breakfast table to have a seat.

Alexandria walked up to her mom and waved her hand in her mom's face. "LANDON GAVE ME A PROMISE RING!" she shouted.

"Stop moving your hand and let me see it!" her mom said excitingly as she grabbed hold of her daughter's hand, looked at the ring and said. "It's beautiful!"

"I know!"

"He has good taste!"

"I know mom. He's so perfect he even got my ring size right!! It fits PERFECTLY!"

"Perfect huh? Or maybe he asked for some help." Her mom chuckled and then said, "He called me a couple of weeks ago and asked for your ring size."

"Mom, you knew about this and you didn't tell me?"

"He said you talked about always wanting a promise ring, and he wanted to give you one. So, I said ok, I guess it's a nice gesture."

"I think it's beautiful!"

"He also dropped this letter off before you got here on his way to work." Alexandria's mom handed her the letter that was sitting on the kitchen table.

"Thank Yoouu," Alexandria said as she grabbed the letter to run upstairs and read it.

Right before she was about to turn around and exit the room, her mom said. "Alex, hold on – let me talk to you for a minute, please."

Alexandria was eager to read the letter, but she knew that she couldn't escape the talk with her mom. So, she walked over to the chair across from where she was sitting, pulled it out and sat down. She looked at her mom and said. "I'm listening...but I just want you to know this is a complete buzz kill."

"I'm aware." her mother responded. "You would tell me if you and that young man were thinking about having sex, right?"

"Mom, this ring has nothing to do with sex. I told you Landon respects my decision to wait until I'm married."

"As much of a relief as that is, sweetie, you know that I want you to be safe, and you're about to be a junior in high school, so you are getting older. I just want to make sure you're careful."

"You know Landon, mom. Please," she said annoyed.

"Alex. I will not sit back and watch you hurt yourself again or end up pregnant. It's my job as your mother to protect you!"

Alexandria grinned sarcastically at her mom. "Great. Much appreciated. Are we done?"

"Actually, I'm not. If I even sense that you are lying to me, it won't be good. Capisce?"

"Mom, it's a ring. A flipping RING - not a proposal!"

"Ok, Alex. I know you know more than me...Rings don't mean much, right?"

"Just be happy for me! Seriously, you have nothing to worry about," Alexandria responded as she reached out to grab her mother's hand and rubbed it to reassure her that all was well.

"Ok. You can go on," her mother finally said.

Alexandria jumped up from the chair and ran up the stairs to her room and closed the door. She plopped down on her bed and opened the envelope. The note read:

Alex,

You're reading this because I found out that you are wearing the ring I gave you. I haven't seen it on you yet, but I would love to, tonight! Pick you up at 7PM?

Love, Landon

Alexandria smiled, picked up her phone and texted Landon:

ALEX:	It's a date ☺
LANDON:	You had me nervous for a second! I thought I wasn't going to hear from you. lol
ALEX:	Had to talk to my MOM!!!!!
LANDON:	Everything must be ok since you are coming.
ALEX:	Yea
LANDON:	Ok. I love you.
ALEX:	☺

Alexandria looked at her phone and smiled. Her heart skipped a beat every time he told her that he loved her. Although Alexandria had yet to say it back, she felt like she did love him. She just wanted to be sure when she said it. She didn't want to say the words 'I love you' to any guy just because he said it to her. She laid there for a couple of minutes until she finally got up to start getting ready for her date.

Alex was nearly done getting ready when she heard a knock on her bedroom door. "Come in!" she yelled.

Steven walked in with a smirk on his face. He took one look at his sister and said, "Dad wants to see you downstairs."

"What are you doing here?" she asked.

"I had some mail that I needed to pick up, and then I heard the news from Mom."

"Oh my gosh! She tells everything! I was going to tell you, honestly."

"No sweat. Where are you all going?"

"He didn't say, and I didn't ask."

"Hmm, well, hurry up and come down."

"OK."

Alexandria's dad was quiet and didn't say much; however, whenever he did have something to say, she took him very seriously. She finished getting ready and rushed down the stairs to see her dad.

Alexandria gave him a hug and said, "Hi, Daddy!"

"Alex, how was your day?" He responded hugging her back.

"It was good. Although, I'm pretty sure mom already told you that Landon gave me this promise ring." Alexandria held out her hand in her father's direction so that he could get a good look at it.

He glanced at the ring and said, "That's nice - behave yourself tonight, you hear?"

"Yes Daddy," she responded. And just like that, he left the room. Alexandria stood there for a second and finally walked into the kitchen where her mom was. "How do I look?" she asked.

"Your mom must be a goddess because you look beautiful," her mom said jokingly.

Alexandria laughed. She heard the doorbell ring and ran to open it. Once the door opened, she laid eyes on Landon.

"Ouue weee, good God. You're beautiful" Landon said as he hugged her. Alexandria loved the way Landon made her feel. It was different than any other guy. She thought to herself '*if this isn't love, I don't know what is.*' And just as soon as she was about to walk out the front door,

Landon stopped her and said. "I can't leave without speaking to your parents Alex; you know that."

As he held out his hand motioning for her to go back inside the house, she turned around and headed for the kitchen.

"Hi, Mrs. Anderson."

"Landon, how was work?"

"It was good. You know they don't let me work many hours during the week because I'm a student, but I make up for it on the weekends."

"Well, that's a good thing. It's to help keep students focused on the fact that school is your first priority."

"Yes ma'am, you're right."

"Where are you all going tonight?"

"Dinner."

"Where Landon? Where are you guys having dinner?"

"Oh, sorry. Arizona's Steakhouse."

"Is that the restaurant by the mall?"

"Yes, ma'am. It's a nice restaurant. I've gone with my dad a couple of times."

"I've never been there, but I don't doubt it. You kids have fun."

"Thank you, Mrs. Anderson."

Alexandria's mom stole a look at her daughter and said. "It's 7 o'clock. You are to be back in this house no later than 10:30pm."

"Got it, Mom. Bye!"

"Drive safely!" Mrs. Anderson yelled as her daughter gripped Landon's hand pulling him towards the front door.

***

Just before she closed the door to lock it, she yelled, "Bye Steven! Bye Daddy!" She didn't wait for a response and shut the door.

The evening was drawing to an end. They had enjoyed a nice romantic dinner. Landon drove as they just listened to music while holding hands. As they got closer to Alexandria's home, she looked over at Landon and said.

"It's kind of early; I don't have to be in the house until 10:30pm...you wanna go hang out at the park for a little while?"

"Ok," he said.

Landon looked over at the clock on the dashboard of his car as he pulled into the park's entrance and it read 9:52.

When he finally pulled into the parking space, he turned off the engine and headlights and said, "Do you want to take a walk?" he asked with a snicker. "I'm guessing no. You are way too gorgeous for that tonight."

She looked at him; happiness was beaming from her eyes as she smiled and said, "You are some kind of different, Landon. Thanks for everything."

"Honestly Alex, you bring this out of me. You're the different one; you march to the beat of this drum on the inside of you, and it's the sexiest thing ever."

Alexandria was touched and then Landon continued. "Ever since I met you, you always talk about real love. I know it's only been six months, but I want that now more than ever. The way that I feel about a girl named Alexandria Anderson is very real."

Alexandria was staring at him but then looked down at her hand and said, "I've been wanting to ask you all night, what do you want me to do with this?"

Looking at her ring, Landon said, "I promise I'm gonna marry you. Not today of course, but wear it until we say 'I do.'"

Alexandria's heart skipped a beat, and she giggled at his confidence. She said, "How in the world do you know at 16 that you're going to marry me?"

Landon never really imagined that the feelings that he had could ever be. But the more time he spent with Alexandria, it made him want to make her fall in love with him even more. He was head over heels, and everyone knew that she had captured his heart by her charm.

He reached over and grabbed her hand, and he looked into her eyes and said. "Because I never want to feel the way I feel about you with another girl. So, I have to marry you. We're soul mates." There was a silence, and then he continued, "Everything about you is perfect, even the things you don't like."

Alexandria had a lot that she didn't like, but she never told him about her insecurities. She never told anyone except her mother and brother for that matter.

They were silent for a while, and Alexandria began to get a little nervous because she didn't know how to respond, so she took her hand back from his. Once they were no longer holding hands, Landon got out of the car and walked over to her door to open it. He held out his hand and felt relieved as she grabbed it. For Alexandria, it was difficult just to say how she truly felt. It was easier to joke around and laugh than deal with serious issues. She would rather ignore it. She had no problem that Landon was so open, in fact, she loved it. Alexandria just had no idea how to open up.

Landon led her out of the car, and then he closed the door. He leaned his back against the passenger car door and pulled her closer to him, wrapping his arms around her. It was gentle, the night was dark, and the lights in the park were dim enough that if you were standing in the right place you could see a few stars. The wind was so light, it almost felt still. They stood there holding one another. Alexandria had her hands draped to her sides as she pressed her head against his chest.

She felt so secure there with him. She trusted him with her heart and knew that out of all the guys she dated in the past, this love was real. Every day, all she could think about was being with Landon, and when they were together, she dreaded when he would have to leave. Alexandria always had a lot to say, but for some reason, she couldn't find words to communicate that moment appropriately.

Landon held her securely for a moment, and then he moved his hands to gently take hold of her chin so that she was looking directly at him. He looked her in the eyes and said, "Alex, I love you."

Right before he was about to lean in to kiss her, she looked into his eyes, she literally felt the world stop moving, and the words slipped through her lips: "I love you too." Right after she released those words, they kissed. A kiss so passionate, a kiss that sealed their deal.

Right underneath the stars in the sky, in the silence of the night, all that was ringing was their love.

CHAPTER 4

Sophomore year had finally ended, and Alexandria spent most of the summer break conditioning for cheerleading, lounging around her house and hanging out at the pool. Of course, whenever Landon wasn't working, they were together.

It was July, and summer break was coming to a close. Alexandria decided to invite a couple of girls over to hang out at the pool. All of the girls hung out a lot when they were younger, but as they got older and their lives changed, they all seemed to go in different directions. They were all still good friends, however, they never really found much time to hang out like they did when they were younger.

All seven girls were sitting on the pool deck eating pizza that hot summer day. Blair, Lauren, and Gia had all been good friends since middle school. Blair and Alexandria had always been close, but they began to drift apart when they both started dating. Lauren and Alexandria were friends, but they just weren't as close as the others. Their relationship became rocky when Lauren immediately started messing around with Nathan after his breakup with Alexandria. Everyone felt there was the unspoken girl code that had been broken and that Lauren was very promiscuous. However, since their moms were good friends, their relationship stayed mutually intact. Gia was the quietest one of all the girls. She was a peacemaker and got along with everyone.

Dianna and Kimberly were Alexandria's childhood friends that grew up with her at church. Dianna was the scholar of the group. She was the go-to girl whenever Alexandria had problems in school and needed extra help. Kimberly was the risk taker. She always hung out with an older crowd which Alexandria's mom didn't care for, but they were practically family.

"Oh, my gosh, Alex! What is that on your finger? I hope you and Landon aren't trying to get married already!?" Kimberly said earnestly, yet jokingly.

"Kim, you are so annoying," Alexandria blasted back, rolling her eyes.

"No, I'm serious! But hey - that's a nice ring girl."

Whitley interjected and said, "She got the ring from Landon. It's his promise to be with her forever."

Whitley had recently broke things off with Randy. She realized that it would be best if she focused on graduating, senior year and colleges. Also, because of the promise she made to her parents and God, her relationship was a huge temptation.

"Whit, you sound mad," Alexandria said without hesitation.

"I mean, she asked!" Whitley responded.

"Well, I think it's sweet!" Dianna said.

Dianna didn't have a boyfriend, but she was always genuinely happy for her friends. Even though she heard all the gossip and the stories behind all the boy drama, she believed that encouraging them to have healthy relationships was important. "Alex, you guys aren't having sex yet. Are you?" Dianna continued.

"Of c-course not--" Alexandria responded.

"But they've talked about it!" Blair blurted out. "Oops. I'm sorry!" she quickly said apologetically.

"Really, Blair? We've talked about marriage too, and that's clearly not happening anytime soon," Alexandria reassured Dianna.

"They aren't having sex; they are just two--young-- love birds," Whitley said in her best friend's defense. She was sitting by Alexandria at the table and nudged her shoulders with her own.

"How long do you plan to wait, girl? The guy is madly in love with you. Pretty soon this 'no sex' game will become old news," Lauren said to Alexandria.

"Thanks, Lauren. But Landon respects my decision," Alexandria answered.

Whitley never really understood why Alexandria remained friends with Lauren. She felt like she didn't deserve the friendship after she had sex with her friend's ex-boyfriend.

Whitley looked in Lauren's direction and told her, "You know Lauren, there's nothing wrong with wanting to wait to have sex. I just recently broke things off with my boyfriend of about two years because he wanted sex and I didn't. Unlike Landon, he just wouldn't respect my decision and kept pressuring me to do something that I wasn't ready to do."

Then Alexandria interjected, "Landon completely understands. He just gets me."

Dianna said, "Alex, it's a beautiful relationship! As long as you're happy, I'm happy for you!"

"Oh, she's happy!" Blair said. All the girls started laughing, and they continued their girl talk around the pool for a couple more hours.

***

School had finally begun, and Alexandria was excited about being considered an upperclassman. Her grades were really good during her freshman and sophomore year, and she intended to keep it that way. Everything in her life was absolutely perfect, and there was nothing that could possibly go wrong.

After a few weeks passed, Alexandria was under a lot of pressure at school. She was beginning to feel overwhelmed. Being stressed out was never a good thing for Alexandria because she handled it by shutting down. She sat in her room frustrated and decided to give Steven a call.

Ring! Ring! Ring! There was no answer, and she did not leave a voicemail. Just as she was hanging up the phone, her mom called her downstairs. She walked down the steps and into the family room where her mom was watching a movie.

"Yes?" she asked her mom.

"Sweetie. Do you want to watch a movie with me?"

"Not really. I have a lot of work to do."

"How's school going?"

"It's fine, mom."

"What's wrong with you? Is everything alright with Landon?"

"Everything is fine with us. I just feel a lot of pressure right now. My grades, competitive cheerleading, training. I just feel like a lot is on my plate."

"Well, let me know if you need any help. This is a crucial year, but it doesn't have to be stressful."

"Thanks..." Alexandria turned around to walk back to her room.

Her mom then said. "Did Steven tell you about his new girlfriend?"

"No, actually he didn't."

"Yea. He brought her by the other day, but you were at practice. A nice girl, you would like her."

"I guess that's why he's not answering my calls?" she said annoyingly and turned to walk back to her room. Her mother sensed that something was wrong, but she didn't want to pry. Once Alexandria got back into her room, she saw that she had two missed calls. One from her brother and the other from Landon. She decided to call her brother back first.

Ring! Ring! Ring!

"Hey, Alex! How's everything going? I saw your missed call."

"I heard you got a new girlfriend."

"Yea, you've actually met her; I just don't think you remember."

Steven could tell something was upsetting his sister, but he also knew that they hadn't talked in a while and wanted to smooth things over before drilling her with questions.

"Oh. Well, mom likes her."

"Yea, she does."

"How's school?" Alexandria asked.

"It's good. Classes are a bit intense now that I am taking classes for my major."

"Same here."

"You can do it, Alex. Why do you sound so down? Is everything ok?"

"Yea."

"How are things with Landon?"

"Everything is fine. I actually missed his call because I was talking to mom so I will give him a call once I get off the phone with you."

"Ok. Well, I will see you around the break, and we will condition for track."

"OK. Bye."

"Bye."

Alexandria was going through a world wind of emotions that she just couldn't shake. After chatting with Landon, she decided that she would go to bed early. When she finally fell asleep, she had a dream that woke her back up around 3 o'clock am. She pulled out her journal, and wrote:

It was the weirdest thing ever. I was underwater, trapped in a bubble that was floating. Then all of a sudden, the water started draining, and I saw my mom. She popped the bubble open and began to dry me off and fix my hair like I was a baby. Then as she held me in her arms, she walked over to a mirror and held me up so that I could see our reflection. When I looked in the mirror, the reflection wasn't mine but a reflection of a much older lady which resembled my great-grandmother. Then my mom kissed the cheek of the woman in the mirror.

When Alexandria finished writing she texted Landon:

ALEX: Are you up?

LANDON: I am now. Another dream?

ALEX: Yea.

LANDON: Do you want to talk about it?

ALEX: No.

LANDON: Are you ok?

ALEX: Yea. Sometimes I feel like the pressure is too much.

LANDON: Babe, 11th grade is hard on everyone.

ALEX: I guess. I'm going to try and go back to sleep.

LANDON: Call me if you need me.

ALEX: You know I have to text. If my mom saw that I was placing calls this late at night, she would take my phone.

LANDON: Ok. Text me. I love you.

ALEX: Love you.

The next morning she woke up before her alarm clock went off. She sat in front of the mirror and just stared at her reflection. Her room was the next door over from her parents, and ever since Alexandria could remember, if she'd listened in the early morning she could always hear her father praying in his closet. She sat there staring and listening. The silence was interrupted moments later by a text message that came in from Whitley.

WHIT:	On my way! 15 min
ALEX:	Ok.

Alexandria hurriedly got dressed as she forgot that her friend was picking her up for school that morning. Once Whitley pulled up, she honked her horn and Alexandria grabbed her books and ran out the front door. As she got in the car, Whitley said, "You forgot?"

"Yea. Sorry."

"It's cool...Also, I wanted to tell you that I talked to Landon a couple of days ago about your anniversary that's coming up."

"Oh really? What about it?"

"He was just trying to get pointers. But I've never asked you what are you planning to get him?"

"Honestly, I don't know. I was thinking about cologne and some shirts. I hope he's not planning anything too big because the ring was enough."

"I don't think it's huge, but I know he's putting thought into it. You know how he is."

"Yea."

They sat there riding in the darkness of the morning for a while and then Whitley said. "You told me the other day you needed help in Spanish. When are you available?"

"Maybe this weekend. Why didn't you warn me that 11th grade would be kicking my butt already?"

"Girl, just stay focused. You know I broke up with Randy my junior year because it was too much to juggle."

"Yea. I remember. It's funny though because Landon is so good in school. He's like a natural."

"You're a natural too girl; you just have a lot of extracurricular activities."

"I need scholarships!"

"Have you decided where you want to go to college?"

"I have a few choices in mind."

"Well, I'm here if you need any help."

"Thanks – Whit. Are you still talking to Liam?" Liam was a freshman in college. They all had gone to high school together, but now he was showing interest in being in a relationship with Whitley.

"Yea, I am. You know now he's off in college in Alabama which I believe will make it difficult, but we'll see. I did want to tell you that I also met this guy named Hayward in basketball camp this summer. He's a senior in high school and goes to a Christian private school in Atlanta."

"So, you completely just stopped talking to Randy?"

"Yea. What's the point, Alex? I mean, I understand there's history there, and I know he's heartbroken over the break-up, but I can't compromise what I believe. It's like I've watched him change over the past couple of months into a person that I don't want to be with, you know? He's started drinking and smoking, trying to fit in during the offseason - but that's not me. So, after I let all of that slide, he still wants me to have sex! And you know how I feel about that. It really shook me up to think about how close I was to actually having sex with him. I just thank God that I was able to take a step back and look at everything, you know?"

"Yea..."

"He said that he was over the whole sex thing, but I just don't really trust him anymore. Sex is something we agreed not to do because of our faith, and our faith was one of the strongest parts in our relationship. Once that was shaken, I just couldn't continue to get caught up in emotions when I know in my heart he's not the right guy for me."

"I guess."

Alexandria understood where Whitley was coming from, but she just didn't want to see their relationship end.

She believed in fighting for what you believe in, especially if love was involved. She spent the rest of the ride to school thinking about her relationship with Landon. She couldn't see herself walking away from someone she loved without giving it all she had. She just felt like Whitley was giving up and choosing to walk away rather than work it out.

CHAPTER 5

After Whitley and Alexandria finally made it to school, Alexandria walked to her first-period class. When she got there, Landon was standing outside the door. As always, she was happy to see his face.

"Hey." she said.

"Hey, Babe. I got you some breakfast."

"Thanks."

"Seems you slept through the rest of the night?"

"Yea."

"That's good," he paused and then said, "You look beautiful."

"I look like crap. I just threw this on," she said giggling.

"You still look beautiful." Alexandria stood there looking at Landon with a blank stare. "So. What do you want to do for our anniversary?" he asked her.

"Nothing extravagant, Landon. Remember, I don't have a job like you. My parents still have to give me money."

"You didn't answer my question," he said.

"I just want to spend it with you."

Landon could tell that Alexandria was becoming more disengaged, and it was starting to bug him that he couldn't figure out why. The bell rung, and they hugged and went their separate ways.

After school, Alexandria had cheerleading practice. When practice was over, she would sometimes ride home with one of her teammates if her mom couldn't pick her up. But today, she had her teammate drop her off at her Aunt Liz's house, who lived in Landon's neighborhood. Once she arrived, she used her key to get in. She was relieved to find that Liz wasn't home. Alexandria gave her a call just to see when she would be getting home, but she didn't answer. Moments later she received a text message from Liz:

AUNTIE:	I'm at work. What's up?
ALEX:	Just calling to see if I could stop by and possibly spend the night.
AUNTIE:	Sure, but I won't be home for a couple of hours so make sure it's ok with your mom.

After that, she texted Landon:

ALEX:	I'm at my aunt's. Can you come over?
LANDON:	Yea. Be there in 5 min.

Then, she texted Mrs. Anderson.

ALEX:	At auntie's house. Can I stay over here tonight?
MOM:	Why?
ALEX:	Because...
MOM:	No.

Last, she texted Steven.

ALEX:	Miss you ☹

She hadn't received a text back from Steven before she heard a knock on the door. Alexandria hurried to open it, and Landon was standing on the other side halfway, out of breath.

"Just finished a marathon?" She jokingly asked.

"No. But I can't stay long," he said, gasping for air. "My mom said it's a school night, and this is the only other night this week I have off-work to catch up on some school work.

"Oh. I have to go home anyways."

"How are you getting home?"

"I don't know. I guess when my mom gets tired of waiting and figures out that my ride dropped me off, she will come and pick me up."

Chuckling and a bit annoyed, Landon said, "You asking for trouble, you know that right?"

"Well, my ride already left!" she shot back as she huffed, rolled her eyes and started to walk away from him.

Landon grabbed her hand and gently pulled her back in his direction and said, "Stop acting like this!"

"Like what?"

"Like you're pissed about something all the time."

"Do me a favor and just be my boyfriend tonight…"

"I just want my girl back."

"I'm right here."

Landon was always able to let Alexandria know when she was going off course a bit, and she loved that about him. He paid close attention to her, and he always responded correctly. She leaned in to kiss him and put her arms around his neck.

"Sooo… you're not having second thoughts about marrying me, right? With my attitude and everything?"

"Girl, you know I love you...attitude and everything."

Landon kissed her and held her waist tightly. Alexandria moved her hand from around his neck and lowered his hands from her waist onto her butt. Then she wrapped her arms around his neck again and brought him closer towards her. Landon was surprised but he didn't say anything. He continued to grab her butt as they were kissing, and she began to walk backward towards the couch. She turned and pushed Landon onto the couch and then Alexandria got on top of him and straddled him.

As they kept kissing on and off, she took off his shirt and then hers. She felt his warm hands on her bare back and it shot what felt like a surge of electricity through her body. Then while they were still kissing, shirtless, she began to unbuckle his belt, and he began to undo her pants as well. She stopped kissing him only for a moment to get up to take her pants off and slid his off as well. Landon was still in the seated position, as Alexandria got back on top of him.

She leaned in to start kissing him again, but then he broke the silence and said, "Alex, Babe, do you know what you're doing?"

"Yes," she replied back.

Then he gently flipped her over on the couch so that she was laying on her back.

"Do you have a condom?" she asked.

"No," he hesitantly replied. There was a pause.

"---it's ok," she said.

Alexandria had never been fully undressed in front of a guy she dated before. She had never gone this far before, but she trusted Landon. As he was unclipping her bra, he asked her, "Are you sure?"

She slipped off her underwear and pulled him closer. As he tried to put it in, he was unsuccessful. He whispered to her, "Babe, you have to relax."

"I'm trying." she said and then began to hold her breath.

He tried again but was unsuccessful. He was beginning to get frustrated, and then he got up and said, "Alex, this isn't right. It doesn't feel right."

"Oh great! So, you can have sex with other people, but you can't have sex with me?"

"It's not even like that; you're just not ready. You know you're not ready!"

"And what the hell does that mean!?" Alexandria became very angry that he just stepped away from one of the most vulnerable moments in their relationship.

"It means, you're not ready."

Landon was a very upset with Alexandria. He couldn't understand what had gotten into her. All he kept thinking was about the time she had messed around with all those guys at that party. He knew this was not what she wanted. As he hurried to put his clothes on, he threw Alexandria her clothes.

"Put 'em on!"

"Really, you're just gonna throw them at me?"

"Yea. I really am."

After Landon got dressed, Alexandria slowly put on her clothes and began to cry. Landon couldn't take it anymore. He wanted to console her, but he didn't know how to get through to her. He wanted to be with her, he wanted to have sex with her, but he didn't want it to be like that. So, he kissed her on her forehead and said, "I gotta go."

He quickly walked out the door and slammed it behind him. Alexandria didn't know what she had done. She didn't know if she was supposed to be mad that he'd left her there crying; or happy that she didn't do something that she would later regret. After she had put her clothes on, she laid on the couch in the silence until she received an incoming call from her dad.

"Hi, daddy," she said, trying to sound cheerful.

"Alex, where are you?"

"I'm at auntie's house."

"I'm outside. It's time to go home."

She met her dad outside. When she got into the car, her dad said, "Alex, you know you're not to be over here when Liz isn't home, especially on a school night, except for emergencies."

"Yes sir," she responded.

As he began to drive home, he asked, "How was your day?"

"It was good. How about you?"

"I'm still blessed and on top of the world."

She rarely said much to her dad, and it was always awkward for her to talk to him. But in the back of her mind, she knew that if there was ever a time when she really needed him, he would be there for her.

When they finally made it home, Alexandria headed straight to her room and shut the door. She checked her phone for any message, and there was nothing. As she got ready for bed and was about to close her eyes, her phone buzzed. She looked at it hoping it was from her brother, but it was from Landon.

LANDON: I love you.

ALEX: I love you too.

That was all they said.

That night she dreamt again. She woke around 3am and began to write in her journal.

> *The dreams keep coming back. Sometimes they are new and sometimes they are ones that I have dreamt before. Tonight I saw a little girl about four years old. She was laying on her back on a closet floor with the lights off, and I felt everything she felt. She was scared because she was in there alone with this guy that was older and cold because her shirt was pulled up. The guy was on top of her. He was kissing her and sticking his huge tongue in her mouth. It was the most disgusting thing ever. He was touching her chest and her private area. She laid there and didn't even fight back. I wanted to fight for her. I felt her wanting to cry, but the tears wouldn't come, it was like it had happened before. When I tried to move him, he wouldn't move. I wasn't strong enough. When I left the closet and walked into the room, I saw other little girls around the same age. I saw guys on top of them too. I felt like I knew them.*

After Alexandria had finished writing in her journal, she looked at her phone, hoping to see a late text from her brother, but there was nothing. So, she texted Landon instead;

ALEX:	Hey
LANDON:	I couldn't sleep either. Sorry about earlier.
ALEX:	Can I call you? I'll use the house phone and make it quick. My mom's a light sleeper.
LANDON:	Ok

Ring!

"Landon. I'm sorry about tonight," she said with tears in her eyes.

"No. It's my fault. I shouldn't have left you like that," he replied.

Alexandria was annoyed that Landon had walked out on her while she was crying. She was annoyed that he had sex with other people but didn't seem to want to have sex with her.

"Still there?" he asked.

"Yea. Landon, why not me? Why don't you want to be with me?"

"I wasn't in love with those other girls. Baby, what we have is real. I don't want to mess that up... But what's really been bothering me is why all of a sudden you wanna have sex?"

She was silent. She didn't know why. She didn't understand a lot of things. Many questions would keep her up at night.

She responded, "I don't know. I just really need *someone*."

"I'm here."

Then there was a click on the line.

"Alex. Get off this phone now!" she heard the voice of her sleepy mom on the other end.

They both quickly hung up the phone. Then Landon text her and said.

LANDON:	I want to know about your dreams.
ALEX:	What about them?
LANDON:	Why you keep having them?
ALEX:	Idk. They aren't scary. Just surreal.
LANDON:	Do you ever dream about me?
ALEX:	Lol. Nope.
LANDON:	So… what do you dream about?

Alexandria loved the fact that she could talk to Landon about anything. She felt at ease when she spoke with him, so peaceful. Her eyes began to get heavy, and she fell asleep before she could even respond.

CHAPTER 6

A few weeks had gone by, and Alexandria celebrated her 16th birthday; her parents gifted her with a new car.

As Alexandria and Landon were getting ready to celebrate their one year anniversary, Alexandria was relieved that it fell on the weekend. That meant she didn't have to live through any embarrassing gifts that Landon might have tried to surprise her with, at school.

On the Saturday morning of their anniversary, Alexandria left her house around 5am and met Landon at the bottom of a local mountain trail. They hiked up the mountain, and when they finally reached the top, they were just in time to see the sunrise. They found a comfortable spot and sat down. They remained there for a while, trying to catch their breath from the hike and take in the beautiful scenery before the silence was broken.

"Wow. I've never done anything like this before." Landon spoke up.

"Me neither," she responded.

When they were making plans on what they would do to celebrate their anniversary, one of the things that they'd planned to do was exchange 365 words of love in the form of a letter. One word was to represent every day they had been together.

Alexandria smiled at Landon. "Did you bring your letter?"

"Yea. I guess I'm going first, huh?" he said nervously as he began to shift in his seated position.

"Yep. That's the plan."

"You can always take it with you…"

"Nice try. I want you to read it to me, and I'll read you mine later," she chuckled.

Landon reached into his pocket and pulled out a folded piece of paper. As he began to unfold his letter, he took a deep breath and then read:

Alexandria, Alex, babe, my one and only, my happily ever after, my forever…words on a paper cannot describe how much I love you. Actions in a day couldn't show it either. Since the day I met you in English class, I knew that there was something unique about you so, when I moved here, I did not want to be here. I missed my friends. I missed my old life, but you helped me look pass that. You helped me to see that I can start a new beginning at a time I felt as though my life was turned upside down. I regretted not choosing to live with my dad as I saw my mom become bitter. I just knew that she needed me to protect her and take care of her. Things between them weren't great. I probably spent more time running away from the drama at home than understanding what was happening. They brought out the worse in each other, but what kid doesn't want their parents together? Every day I spend with you, I learn something new about myself. Like, how even though my parents got a divorce, it doesn't mean that I cannot find true love. I know there is so much more to you, and I honestly can't wait to learn all that there is to know. You make everything in my life a million times better. You are so fine and so sexy. You are truly the apple of my eye. You are my everything. I know that you say that we are young, but I couldn't imagine spending the rest of my life with anyone else other than you. My ultimate goal in life is to make you smile. I love everything about you. I love your laugh. I love your hair. I love the way your skin smells. I love the way you walk. I love the way you talk. I am so in love with you. You make me a better man. You are my best friend, my rib, my soul mate, my other half. You are one of a kind. I wish that we could fly away, and I would take you to Utopia.

After Landon finished reading Alexandria the letter, he looked at her and asked, "What do you think?"

"It was perfect," she said, smiling as she leaned over and gave him a kiss on the cheek.

They sat there staring at the horizon. Landon holding Alexandria in his arms, until finally, Landon broke the silence again by admitting he was hungry. They headed down the mountain and found a cozy breakfast spot that was nearby. After breakfast, they were walking back to their cars, and Landon said to Alexandria, "I know you didn't want me to be too much and I respect that, but I got you something..."

"Landon! What is it?" she said, surprised.

Landon opened his car door, reached into the glove compartment and pulled out a jewelry box.

"Oh my gosh!! Babe. Really?"

"I saw it when I got you the promise ring, and I've been saving to get it for you since then."

Alexandria took the box and opened it. Inside was a sterling silver necklace with a diamond pendant.

"Wow. It's beautiful!" she said, moving the box back and forth so that the diamond sparkled in the reflection of the sun.

"I was going to give it to you later, but I figured I could just give it to you now and you can wear it later."

Alexandria leaned in to give Landon a tight hug and kissed him on the lips, then asked, "Speaking of later, what time do you get off work?"

"I get off tonight around 6:00, so let's meet up at 7:30."

Alexandria leaned into Landon to give him another kiss on the lips and said, "Thank you for the necklace. I will definitely wear it later." Flashing him a smile while looking deep into his eyes.

As they pulled away from each other, they both got into their cars, and Landon headed home to get ready for work. Alexandria had a couple of hours to spare before she would start getting ready to see him again, so she decided to head over to Whitley's house. As she pulled into the driveway and parked her car, she sat there for a while, smiling and staring at the necklace before she put it on. Then she reached into her cup holder to grab her phone and call Steven.

After a few rings, she got Steven's voicemail. She decided not to leave a message but sent him a text instead.

ALEX: Just wanted to say Hi.

To her surprise, he responded.

STEVEN: Hey Alex! Sorry I missed your call. In the library right now. Miss you and will see you on break.

Alexandria was excited to finally hear from her brother. She quickly responded.

ALEX: I was beginning to think you forgot about me.

STEVEN: Not a chance, kid.

ALEX: Good! When do you get back?

She waited for a few minutes, but Steven didn't respond. When she didn't hear right back from him, she knew that it would probably take a while. She got out of her car and walked around Whitley's house to the side door. She didn't see Whitley's car, but she knocked anyways, and Whitley's little sister answered.

"Hey, Alex!"

"Carey, Hey! Is Whit home? I didn't see her car outside, but I thought I'd check anyways."

"Yea, come in. My dad took her car for a checkup," she said, leading Alexandria into the kitchen. "She's in her room. But I will warn you, she's cranky." She rolled her eyes, shook her head and walked away.

"Thanks," Alexandria said hesitantly. She walked upstairs towards Whitley's room and knocked.

"WHAT DO YOU WANT NOW?!" Alexandria heard Whitley yell from behind the door.

"Uh-Whit. It's me, Alex," she chuckled.

"Oh!"

Whitley swung open the door. "Sorry, Carey has been bugging me all morning about borrowing my shirt," Whitley said as she walked back to her closet to continue organizing it.

"It's cool. I would've called, but I was on my way home so I thought I'd swing by."

"How was the hike?"

"It was good. When we were halfway up, I started to regret the idea," she giggled.

"I told you. Was it cold?"

"Yea, a little. Landon was all like, DON'T QUIT ON US NOW!"

Alexandria laughed as she explained the morning events while walking over to Whitley's desk to pull out the chair. Whitley laughed at her friend.

"Then he read his letter that I told you we were writing to each other. It was very sweet and then turned borderline corny when he started talking about Utopia."

"Utopia? What the heck is that?" She stopped and looked at Alexandria who was sitting at her desk.

"Your guess is as good as mine. I just didn't want to ruin it," she giggled.

"You're awful."

"Well, I need to figure out where it is because that's where he wants to take me."

They both laughed. Then Whitley said, "Have you finished your letter?"

"Yea."

"I have to hear!" she said as she continued organizing her clothes.

"Well, I don't have it with me. But trust me when I say it's good."

"What do you'll have planned for tonight? I know you said you wanted to keep it low-key."

"Nothing really. Just going over to my auntie's. He's working during the day, but we are probably just going to watch a movie. I told him I just wanna to be with him. But speaking of trying to keep it low-key, look at what he bought me!" Alexandria showed Whitley the necklace that was around her neck.

"Oh my gosh! Alex. It's gorgeous! He always gets you the best gifts. Where'd you find him?" she joked.

"I have no idea."

"What did you end up getting him?"

"Luckily a watch. I didn't wanna to do too much, but I'm glad I didn't go with the shirts," she laughed.

"He really goes over and above. What did Steven say?"

"He doesn't know...He's been so detached lately."

"Oh, yea. You told me he has a new girlfriend and busy with school, right?" Whitley stopped and looked in Alexandria's direction as she could tell the topic bothered her best friend.

"Yea. I wish I could tell you more, but that's all I know. I don't really know this girl, and she's already annoying."

"Really, Lex..."

"Don't get me wrong. I want my brother to be happy but..."

"You're being mean and unfair. Your attitude towards Steven isn't right. Cut him some slack; he's away at college, you know?" Whitley said, trying to reassure her friend. She knew that Alexandria missed Steven, but she could tell she was resenting the fact that he left and had another girl in his life other than her. Whitley continued, "I'm pretty sure he's busy with other important things besides a girlfriend."

"I guess," Alex said, still annoyed at the situation.

"Not EVERYONE is boy crazy!" Whitley said as she folded her arms looking at Alexandria.

"Wow, Whit. YOOOUU of all people think I'm boy crazy?" She sarcastically chuckled. "I would say you're jealous!" She said annoyed at Whitley, rolling her eyes.

"Jealous, Alex? Get real. You're freaking kidding yourself if you really believe that your relationship with Landon hasn't consumed you."

"Sounds like you have a problem," she shot back.

"Ok - just forget I said anything."

"Yea. How about we do that."

Alexandria was furious. How could Whitley feel that way about her? Couldn't she see that Landon made her happy? How could she not see how Steven just deserted her to fight for herself? He might have been away at school, but she wasn't used to him not being around or one call away. And now her best friend wasn't being supportive. Alexandria didn't want to seem childish about the situation, so she sat there making small talk until it was a good time for her to go without it seeming awkward.

CHAPTER 7

Alexandria made it home from Whitley's when she received a phone call from Landon. He was taking a break.

"Hey, Babe," he said.

"Hey. I miss you."

"I miss you too. What've you been up to?"

"Nothing really. I went over to Whit's for a while and then came home."

"Cool. How is…"

"Oh yea," she interrupted, "I talked to Steven today."

"That's good. How is he?"

"I guess he's good. It was short. He's busy with school and stuff."

"Oh ok. I know he's making big moves, being the big man on campus. That's really good for him," Landon joked.

"Yea. I guess."

"So, will your aunt be home tonight?"

"Yea. But she knows that we are coming over so she said she would just be in her room."

"Ok, cool. I've gotta go, but I'll see you tonight," Landon quickly added.

"Ok," Alexandria said, and they both hung up.

Alexandria spent a little time perfecting her letter to Landon. Then she spent the rest of the time getting prepared for the night.

She drove over to Liz's house a little early, and once she arrived, she went inside and began talking to her aunt. Moments later, Mrs. Anderson arrived.

"Mom. What are you doing here?"

"Oh, I'm sorry. You must have forgot that this is *my* sister's house."

"I know that. But Landon and I are hanging out here tonight!"

"The place is big enough for everyone, Alex, stop being dramatic."

Alexandria was upset that Mrs. Anderson showed up unannounced, especially when Mrs. Anderson knew that she was hanging out there on that particular night. She thought to herself, *we could have just hung out at home if we knew you were going to show up*. Then her mom added, "If you weren't just going through your daily routine as if you don't live with your parents and actually took the time out to talk to me, then you would've known that I'd be here."

"Whatever, mom. You're doing this on purpose," Alexandria hissed. Then she texted Landon.

ALEX:	My mom is here so I'll meet you outside.
LANDON:	Ok.

When Landon finally arrived, Alexandria ran to meet him with a hug and a kiss, as he was at the curb walking up the driveway.

"We're not going in," she told him.

"Alex, I have to say something to your mom. Do you want her to hate me?" Landon said. Alexandria huffed and led him towards the front door.

Once she got to the door, she turned around to face him and said, "We're not staying inside. We're going for a walk."

"Ok," he responded and kissed her on the forehead.

Alexandria opened the front door and led him into the kitchen where Mrs. Anderson and Liz were seated, having a conversation and eating.

"Hey, mom! Hey, auntie! How are y'all doing tonight?" Landon said walking over to them with open arms to give them a hug.

"Fine. Nice to see you again," Mrs. Anderson responded as she returned the hug. Landon walked over and gave Liz a hug as well. "Alex is throwing a tantrum about me being here, but we'll be here in the kitchen so you guys can have the living room." Mrs. Anderson said to Landon, trying to ease the tension she was sensing from her daughter.

"Oh. That's fine! We're gonna take a walk, but we will come back in later on if that's alright?"

"That's fine," Mrs. Anderson said.

While Landon was wrapping up his conversation with Mrs. Anderson, Alexandria slipped away to go and unlock the back door to the basement. When she finally got back, Landon asked her if everything was ok. She told him that she had forgot to do something but everything was fine.

As they were holding hands, walking and just enjoying each other's company and conversation,

Alexandria asked Landon, "Are you ready to hear my letter?"

Landon responded, "Yea, I've been waiting all day. But I can take it with me since we're walking. I'd much rather focus on you."

"Well, let's head back to the house then. I left the back door unlocked to the basement, so they won't know that we're there. It's an unfinished basement, but it's a work in progress. There's a guest bedroom that's full of stuff. It may be crowded, but we can have some privacy."

"Ok. Let's do that."

"Oh, yea - and make sure you put your phone on vibrate," Alexandria told Landon.

When they finally got to the back door, they snuck in quietly and locked the door behind them. Once they were in the room, they sat on the floor with their backs against the wall that was closest to the window. Alexandria laid her head on Landon's shoulder. Then he said, "You sure we're ok back here?"

"Of course," She assured him.

He asked her for the letter. She had it folded in her back pocket. She reached for it and asked him if he wanted to read it himself or if she could read it to him. He told her that she could read it. She repositioned herself so that she was seated on the floor, Indian-style, directly facing him.

He smiled at her and joked, "If you see water around my eyes when you're done reading, I'm sweating."

He was giggling and then she responded, "You have high expectations. I don't want to disappoint you..." She laughed, swallowed and shook away some of the jitters she was feeling. However, she knew that the words that she'd written would only sound right coming directly from her.

Alexandria read:

To my forever and a day, my boo, my sweetheart, my one and only, my good guy. You are something special. Everything about you is perfect. Sometimes too perfect to the point that I don't understand how I got so lucky. You are the most understanding guy I know. You listen to my every word, and you pay attention to my every detail. You complete me. You know exactly what to say to turn every frown into a smile. You are simply the best. I have never loved anyone the way that I love you. I have never told anyone that I loved them. I've been in puppy love but never this. The hardest things that I've gone through within this past year seems like nothing because you were right there. You are too good to me. I will forever cherish the love that we have. My past is not the easiest to grasp, and sometimes I myself cannot even grasp it. You make me feel like the only girl in the world, and I will forever be your one and only. When I am with you, everything makes sense. I can escape some of my biggest fears every time you are near. You know exactly when to touch me and where to touch me. Your sweet kisses on my forehead makes me feel like a princess. You shower me with the most precious gifts; you are killing me softly. Thank you for always having my back. Thank you for always looking out for my best interest. Thank you for respecting my decisions. Thank you for being that guy. I never thought that someone like you could be, and now I can say that I will marry my high school sweetheart. My first true love and my only. Thank you for teaching me how to love. Thank you for loving me. We can only go up from here. There is no one I would rather spend the rest of my life with other than you. You are the air I breathe. Never leave me because baby I honestly need you to survive. I need you to know that I am so in love with you.

After Alexandria finished reading the letter to Landon, she felt another release of weight lifted off her shoulders. She had never been so vulnerable about her feelings before. She didn't wait for him to say anything. She moved closer to him and leaned in to give him a kiss, first on the lips, then on the cheek. Then she whispered in his ear, "I-Want-You."

She had been thinking about this for a while. Having sex with Landon was the only thing she thought about. She figured since they were going to be together forever, why wait. She thought that there would be a rebuttal from him, so she waited. But to her surprise, he whispered back in her ear, "I-Want-You-Too." He gently grabbed her neck and began to kiss her.

It was dark in the room. One couldn't see much except for what the exterior house light illuminated in the room. Many thoughts were racing through Alexandria's head. She couldn't slow her thoughts down.

As they both began to undress, they were kissing and touching. She had never done this before, but it seemed to flow. She figured whatever she didn't know or didn't do right, Landon would tell her. She was in the moment physically, but her mind was racing, racing, racing.

Then the question popped in her head, *what are you doing Alex? What will Steven say if he finds out?* Then she answered *he loves me.* At that moment, she realized that she was on the floor on her back. Her legs were opened, and there Landon was in between her thighs. She didn't feel a thing; she was numb. *Was this what everyone talks about?* She thought.

Then Landon leaned down towards her and said, "You know I love you, right?" Alexandria didn't respond. This was what she thought she wanted, but she didn't feel the way she thought it was supposed to make her feel.

She loved him, and she wanted to feel closer, but three minutes later, Landon pulled out as he was about to climax. Alexandria happened to look down, and from the light shining through the window, she could see some blood was on his hand. He took his undershirt, which he had positioned under them, and began to clean himself, and he attempted to clean Alexandria as well. She sat up to put back on her clothes. She looked at him and smiled. Alexandria wanted to see if the love that she always felt was in his eyes was still there. He seemed happy.

He stood up, while putting his clothes back on with one hand and reached out the other to help her up. She hadn't felt much, but when she stood up, she realized something did happen. When they were fully dressed, Alexandria just wanted to be in Landon's arms, but Landon wanted them to get out of the house. She followed him as they quietly made their way out the back door. He had balled up the undershirt and placed it in a trash bag that was tied inside the garbage bin on the side of the house. They walked around to the front of the house; he left Alexandria outside as he went in to use the bathroom and wash his hands. He returned to her as quickly as he had left.

It grew dark out, and it was now a little after 9:00PM. Landon sat on the highest step on the front porch and motioned for Alexandria to sit between his legs on a lower step. He held her and then kissed the side of her cheek and whispered in her ear. "Alex, baby. You just lost your virginity."

She smiled and said, "I gave it to you." She was at peace with her decision. They were together now, and that was all that truly mattered.

A few minutes later, Ms. Anderson opened the front door and was getting ready to leave and said to Alexandria, "I was just getting ready to call you. I'm about to leave. Can you help me bring some of those bags on the kitchen counter out to my car?" Alexandria immediately got up and walked as fast as she could to the kitchen to get the bags and followed her mom. When Mrs. Anderson was settled in the car, she turned to Alexandria and said. "I expect you to be home soon," Alexandria said ok and began to walk away as normal as she possibly could.

Mrs. Anderson called her back to the car. "Why are you walking like something is between your legs? Like you just had sex or something?"

"Really, Mom?" Alexandria said irritated, trying to blow off her mom's intuition. "I've just been sitting down for a long time!" She quickly stormed off away from her mom.

It was in that moment that she realized that she and Landon had to be in this together. It was in that moment that she realized that they had to work out. It was in that moment that she realized that she would do anything to keep his love. It was in that moment that she realized that he was the only guy that she ever wanted to be with.

Once Alexandria got home, she took a hot shower and got ready for bed. She then called her childhood friends, Dianna and Kimberly. When they were all on the three-way call, she said, "I want you ladies to be the first to know that as of tonight, I am no longer a virgin."

Alexandria wanted to tell Whitley, but she knew Whitley would not understand since she broke up with her boyfriend because she didn't want to have sex. Dianna and Kimberly never had sex before, but they weren't opposed to it. They were shocked, but they expected it since Landon and Alexandria had become so close. They laughed about it, pointing out that Kimberly would be next. As Alexandria hung up the phone with them, she answered the incoming call from Landon.

"Hey, baby."

"Hey," he said, "I just wanted to make sure that you were ok."

"Yea. I'm ok," she responded.

"Alex, can you believe we just had sex?"

"I know, right? But I love you."

"Love you too."

***

They stayed up talking on the cell phone a little longer that night. Landon and Alexandria continued to grow closer together, and they continued to have more and more sex. They were consumed with one another, and nothing else seemed to matter.

Liz was staying over at their house in the guest bedroom. Landon and Alexandria had sex in there several times when her parents weren't home. Alexandria was always careful to clean up afterwards; however, it seems that one particular time they forgot a condom wrapper under the pillow. Liz brought what she found under the pillow to her sister's attention. A few days later, Mrs. Anderson demanded a sit-down talk with her daughter.

As they were sitting in the kitchen, Alexandria's mom asked: "Are you having sex?"

"No, mom."

"Alex, Liz found this condom wrapper in the guest bedroom, and it's not from me and your father. Now, I want you to be honest with me. Because if I find out that you're lying to me, you know there will be more consequences."

There was no one else, except her, that the condom could belong to if it didn't belong to her parents. No one else lived in the house. Quickly Alexandria said, "Ok. It's mine. But we didn't have sex! We tried to, but it didn't work."

Mrs. Anderson was pretty lenient with Alexandria, especially with her being the youngest, but not lenient enough for her 16-year-old daughter to be having sex in her house and lie about it. "Ok, Alex," Mrs. Anderson replied, "I am scheduling an appointment with my doctor, and if I find out that you're lying and you are sexually active, you're going to be in more trouble than you are right now. So, you better tell me the truth before we get there."

Alexandria didn't know what to do. If she told her mom the truth, she would get in trouble. If she lied, her mom would find out, and she would still get in trouble.

The next day, Mrs. Anderson scheduled an urgent appointment with her gynecologist; however, before they left for the appointment that morning, Alexandria decided to tell her the truth, that she was having sex with Landon.

"How long has this been going on?"

"Just that one time, Mom."

"Alex, you've already lied. I don't trust anything that is coming out of your mouth at this point. What if you're pregnant?"

"I'm not."

"How do you know? Huh? Tell me!?" her mom shouted frantically.

"I don't…"

The car ride wasn't the best; Mrs. Anderson was furious. She was so furious it seemed like she was calling everyone to embarrass Alexandria: her dad, her brothers, her sisters, her aunts.

At the gynecologist's office, Mrs. Anderson requested the doctor put Alexandria on birth control pills. After they left the office, Mrs. Anderson said, "Give me your phone and your car keys! Alex, you and this young man need to take a break, do you understand?"

"Yes…" she responded sorrowfully.

The truth was that Alexandria didn't understand. This was her soul mate, and her mother was ruining her life. She couldn't understand why she would place her on birth control and demand her to leave him alone. She didn't understand why she would make the only person who ever cared about her disappear, all because she didn't agree with the timing or the way things happened. She thought to herself, *if anything, my mother should be happy that I didn't lose my virginity when she did. She should be grateful that I chose to wait a little longer.*

What Alexandria thought didn't matter. That night, she laid on her bed and cried herself to sleep.

CHAPTER 8

The next morning, when Mrs. Anderson dropped Alexandria off at school, and she immediately went to find Landon.

"Landon! Landon!" she yelled once she had spotted him in the library with a few of his friends. Landon could see she was upset; he quickly got up, grabbed his things and walked out to divert the situation. Alexandria followed him.

"So, you were just going to hide from me, you weren't even going to wait by my locker?"

"Alex, calm down."

"What do you mean calm down?" She could barely breathe, she was getting hot, and she could feel the tears beginning to swell in her eyes.

"Alex."

"So, you're done?"

"Alex, your parents came to my house late last night

and told my mom that I wasn't allowed to talk to you anymore. I can't talk to you, at least for now."

"You don't mean that! You said you loved me!" There was no response. "Landon!?" She was trying not to cause a scene, but she wanted to scream at the top of her lungs.

"Of course I love you. But we can't do it like this; we gotta wait it out."

"We are at school Landon. What the hell are you scared of?"

"Let's just cool it off for now. I'll talk to your parents, I promise."

"I want to be with you now."

Landon's intentions when he first started dating Alexandria was never to break her heart, but he didn't see any other way out at the moment and responded, "I'm sorry Lex, but that's not an option. We'll get through this though."

"Wow – Unbelievable." She looked at Landon with disgust, "I guess you got what you wanted, huh? Time to cash out with the boys?"

She couldn't believe what was happening, "So much for sticking together!" She turned around and hurried away.

***

The next couple of weeks were very hard for Alexandria. She couldn't afford not to be focused, and Mrs. Anderson knew that the added stress wouldn't be good for her daughter. She decided that she would try and talk to Alexandria herself. She knocked on the bedroom door and opened the door to find Alexandria lying down.

"Alex… Alex!… Alexandria!"

"Huh?"

"You do know that I can only help you if you talk to me? Sweetheart, you have to pull yourself together."

"Mom, why are you doing this to me?" she asked with tears in her eyes.

"Alex. I'm trying to help, sweetheart, but you won't talk to anyone."

"I don't want to talk to anyone. The only person that I want to talk to, you banned him from my life. Mom, why?"

"If he really wanted to talk to you Alex, he would. Don't fool yourself into thinking that he's distant because of this. You both needed space."

"No. We were fine."

"Why aren't you taking Steven's calls?"

"Steven doesn't care, Mom!" she yelled.

"Alexandria Anderson, if you don't pull yourself together, you will be in summer school. And if you end up there, you can forget about a senior year with Landon or your future at that. And if you won't talk to us, I will go ahead and make an appointment for you to talk to Dr. Robinson again. I'm sure he will be surprised but more than happy to help."

Ms. Anderson walked out of the room, and Alexandria sat there gathering all the strength she had to push through the 1st semester of her junior year.

***

The second half of the year came in and Alexandria placed all her energy into her schoolwork. She decided that since cheerleading was over, she wouldn't do track this year – that way she could balance her time better. However, she still wasn't able to talk to Landon. She spent a lot of time on her outfits and make-up daily, making sure that she looked her best. But, she rarely ever ran into Landon because they didn't have any classes together. Alexandria still had hope that they would eventually get back together.

The break-up between Landon and Alexandria was all over school, and everyone was becoming more comfortable with the idea but still wanting to know what really happened. Justin, Alexandria's ex, and her were still friends even though their relationship didn't work. Their lockers were near each other. At the end of school one day, Justin decided that he would talk to Alexandria for a minute just to see how she was doing.

"Hey, Heartbreaker," he said jokingly with her as he walked up to her locker.

"Hey. What's up, Justin?"

"Nothing much. How are you?"

"I'm good… Ready for senior year so I can be one year closer to getting up outta here. You know?" She was placing her books in her locker.

"Yea, I know what you mean." There was a brief pause. "Alex, you sure you're alright?"

"Of course. Why?"

"You just haven't been yourself lately. You've been all to yourself; you haven't even been to a basketball game to see anyone or even Whit, you know it's her senior year, right?"

"I didn't think I was bothering anyone," she responded sarcastically.

"I mean, no one asked me to come over here, I just decided to check-in with an old friend. Making sure you're ok."

"Thanks for doing that, honestly. I'm good though. My grades slipped last semester, and I just want to make sure my grades are ok this semester to pull my GPA up."

"I understand. Are you running track this year?"

As she closed her locker, she looked at him standing there and said, "Nope. I haven't really been training, and I doubt I'll be able to with my grades and my parents on my back 24/7."

"That sucks - We're going to miss you out there, but I get it. Well, at least come out and see one game this year. The season will be over before you know it."

"I'll try," she said as she shot him a quick smile and turned to walk down the hallway out the double doors that led outside.

Once she was outside, she saw Landon who seemed to be waiting for someone.

"Hey, Alex!"

Her heart started racing really fast; she hadn't spoken to Landon in a couple of months. "Hey," she responded.

"Headed to your car?"

"No. I'm waiting for my mom."

"Still no car?"

"Nope, but I do happen to have my phone," she said annoyed. She didn't know how Landon expected her to act when he brushed her off when she tried to reach out to him when everything first happened. The more she thought about what her mom said over the past couple of weeks, it angered her that Landon had not even attempted to contact her.

"What's that supposed to mean?"

"It means, why haven't you called or at least texted?"

"Oh, I get it, you think this is easy for me?"

"Well, if it isn't, you sure do put up a good front," she said, walking quickly towards the parking lot. Landon followed and cut in front of her. He reached for her hand and led her off to the side of the school near some empty trailers.

Alexandria was angry with Landon. She had put all her trust in him, and he let her down. She didn't want to deal with him or anyone else for that matter. She didn't understand what happened that caused him to change his mind because she was always willing to fight for their relationship. She was in love with him and had given him her heart.

She pulled her hand away once they were secluded and asked, "Did you even try to talk to my parents like you promised, huh? ---No. You were too busy "kickin' it" with your boys. If I was holding you down from something, you could've told me that from day one."

Alexandria was annoyed with Landon. She felt like their relationship was secure enough that if Landon had taken the time to hang with his friends, it would have been ok.

"Who the hell do you think you are? You think you're the only one with feelings?" he said angrily

"It sure seems that way," she said turning to walk away. Landon hurried to run in front of her and grabbed both of her arms and pushed her back into the trailer. "You think I didn't see that stunt with you in the hallway flirting with Justin?"

Alexandria was shaken up. Her backpack had braced her from getting hurt. Landon had never been forceful with her before. But the only thing that she thought was that *he must still have feelings for me or else he wouldn't be this upset.* Landon quickly released her as he noticed the frightened look on her face. Alexandria couldn't find any words to say. A million thoughts began to race through her mind. All she wanted to do was get out of there before anyone saw them. Landon looked at her waiting for her to say something, and with a world of mixed emotions, she walked away quickly towards the parking lot to find her mom's car.

Alexandria made it home and settled in. She was trying to finish up homework with countless thoughts racing through her mind. She didn't understand why Landon didn't try harder. She also didn't understand why he was so upset when nothing happened with Justin. She didn't understand why he didn't want to be with her. She didn't understand why she had no one to talk to.

As the thoughts kept racing, her cell phone started to ring.

Ring! Ring! Ring! Ring! Ring!

Alexandria looked at the screen. It was Landon. Her heart started racing as she got anxious and nervous all at the same time. It was the first time in months that he had called her.

"Hello?" she said confused.

"Hey, Alex. I'm in your neighborhood, a few houses up. Can you come out so we can talk?"

"Umm, yea. Give me a couple of minutes."

She hung up, pulled herself together, and headed outside. When she got outside, Landon was already there. His car was sitting out front. She approached Landon's car, as he got out and positioned himself with his back on the car so that he was facing her. They didn't greet each other with an embrace. Alexandria was extremely nervous because she had no idea what to expect.

"Alex. I'm sorry for earlier," Landon said. "I just have a lot going on." Alexandria wanted to say something, but she didn't know what to say. Landon took a step towards Alexandria, he asked, "You know I love you, right?"

Alexandria nodded. She was quiet, and everything in her wanted Landon to embrace her and tell her that, despite everything, they should still be together. As Landon stepped closer, she got butterflies in her stomach, and she felt as if she was going to throw up. He reached out to embrace her, and she calmed down enough to be in the moment. Tears began to swell up in her eyes as her head rested on his chest. She squeezed him tight just to make sure it was real. They stood there for a moment with tears rolling down Alexandria's face. She started to sniffle, and he held her a little tighter.

Alexandria wanted to go on as if nothing happened, but deep down inside she knew that a lot had changed. She didn't move, but she found the courage to ask, "Why didn't you call me?"

"Alex, I got caught up."

"Caught up with what?"

"I was hurt too. When your parents told me I couldn't talk to you anymore, I didn't know what to do, and I didn't know how you would react or what you had told them."

"I get it, but I at least tried to talk to you. You didn't even try," she said pulling away from him as the tears continued down her cheeks. "You said you would talk to my parents, you never did."

"They were pretty upset with me, Lex."

"Well, what did you expect? You're the guy that had sex with their teenage daughter!" She said as she wiped the tears away. It seemed as though all the emotions started to build at once. She was happy to see Landon; sad that things felt different; angry that it took him so long to reach out to her and anxious for them to get back together.

"Let's just forget about everything that happened. My parents will be ok. I just want to be with you," she finally said, looking into his eyes.

"Alex, it isn't that easy."

"What's wrong? Why don't you want to be with me anymore?"

"Alex…"

Landon appeared to have something to say. Alexandria could tell by the look on his face that it was important. It seemed as though everything was up in the air.

"I'm with someone else," he finally said.

And at that moment when Landon released those words, it seemed as though the world came crashing onto her chest. She closed her eyes really tight as she felt the ground beneath her spin; she nearly fell trying to walk away. Then she stopped once she was in front of her house and looked at Landon. He looked sorrowful, as though he never wanted Alexandria to feel the way he knew she felt.

With rage and the tears beginning to flow even more than before, she whispered out loud enough for him to hear. "How could you?" She placed her hand on her heart as if to stop it from coming out of her chest, and fell to her knees into the grass. Landon got into his car and drove off. As she watched and the tears flowed, she began to dig a hole in the dirt. She looked at her hands and saw the promise ring that she was still wearing. She took it off and placed it in the hole and buried it. And at that moment, she knew it was over.

CHAPTER 9

Alexandria and Whitley rarely talked after she started having sex with Landon, and it seemed as though they naturally went separate directions after she graduated. Alexandria had become very distant, and she knew that she had things going on that Whitley wouldn't agree with. So much had happened that she didn't know how to explain it all. Whitley had attempted to reach out to Alexandria several times, but she just wasn't ready to face the reality that it really was time to let go of her dreams of forever after and move on with her life.

The school year had ended, and Whitley finally graduated. Alexandria attended the graduation ceremony and went to a few graduation parties, but she was really disengaged from everything that was going on. She heard that Landon was no longer with the girl that he told her about, but it was easy to deal with them being together because she didn't attend their school.

Alexandria spent most of her summer working out and training for the upcoming competitive cheerleading season. She did enjoy being with her teammates at practice because it took her mind off of everything that was going on around her. One day at cheer practice, one of her teammates told her that while she was at a local electronics store, she saw Landon, and he told her how he'd changed jobs and had a new girlfriend. Alexandria didn't mind the news; she had become numb to all the latest updates. She told herself that she wouldn't believe it until she either saw it or heard it from him herself.

She recognized that she was still having issues controlling her emotions, so she made the decision to go back to the family counselor. Most of the time, Alexandria would just sit and stare off in Dr. Robinson's office. She just enjoyed having someone there.

"Alex, you know that you have your whole life ahead of you?"

She didn't respond. Dr. Robinson waited a moment and said, "Let's talk about what has happened between the last time you were here until now." Alexandria still didn't respond. This wasn't the first session with Dr. Robinson that summer. But Alexandria felt more comfortable when they were just talking about her feelings, than dealing with facts.

At the end of their time together that day, he told her that if there was anything that she wanted to say, write it in her journal and bring it back. Alexandria left his office with so much to say but not truly understanding where to begin or even how to get it out.

Everyone knew how serious Landon and Alexandria had become, and when things came to an abrupt end, people also saw how difficult it was for Alexandria to move on. For the first time in a long time, Alexandria had nowhere to run to find a distraction or rebound. She did, however, find peace in being in the presence of Dr. Robinson, even if she didn't always have something to say. He was patient and consistently invested in her best interest, and she appreciated that. Every week, she continued her sessions.

"How has it been, Alex?" Dr. Robinson asked during the next session.

"Ok. I was going to write but I couldn't."

"Why not?" he asked.

"I don't know," she responded. "I just didn't know how to write it down."

"Your writing is good. I believe it will come to you when you least expect it," Dr. Robinson said.

They talked about cheerleading and all the general things that she felt comfortable talking about. Then he asked.

"You remember when you told me that you used to have these dreams? Do you still have them?"

"Not every day," she said, "but from time to time."

"Are you still journaling them like we talked about?"

"Most of them," she responded.

"How about you tell me about them, maybe we can try to understand them together?"

Alexandria was hesitant because she didn't talk to anyone about her dreams. They were weird to her and not something she could go around telling people about; however, she did tell Dr. Robinson about the incident with the guys during middle school, so she knew that her dreams were safe with him. She took a deep breath and decided to talk to him about them.

"Well, in the most recent dream, I was dressed very beautifully. My hair and nails were done, and I had a custom-made dress on. When I saw myself, I was actually so shocked that I didn't recognize myself. My entire family was there; they looked nice too. It seemed as though we were celebrating something, but I don't know what, and there were other people there that I didn't know.

Then there was this older man, who I really felt like I did know. I just couldn't make out who he was. He was literally pulling me into a corner while everyone wasn't paying attention. We were all in the same room, but they just didn't notice. The music was so loud that even if I tried to scream, you couldn't hear me. I started to pull away, and he grabbed me again and pulled me into a side room. He locked the door, and I stumbled on my dress and fell down. He quickly started to unbuckle his pants. I could tell he was drunk. He pulled out his private part and was walking closer to me as he told me to just touch it. I managed to quickly get up, and dodged him as I ran as fast as I could out of the room. I ran all the way through the crowd to the back entrance and out the door onto the deck where I saw a pool. Without even thinking I jumped into the body of water fully dressed and stayed underwater holding my breath for as long as I could."

Alexandria stopped and looked over at Dr. Robinson.

"Interesting. Did you feel scared at all?" Dr. Robinson asked.

"No. Not really. I just wanted to get away from him."

"Do you think this dream has any meaning?"

"Uuhh. No, I don't think so."

There was silence. Alexandria was thinking, *of course, it doesn't mean anything. Nothing ever means anything. Everyone does whatever they want, whenever they want.*

"You know," she said, trying to move past the dream into what was really bothering her. "I heard that my ex, Landon, has a new girlfriend."

"How does that make you feel?" he asked.

"Like throwing up." she joked, "And then I feel nervous and scared all at the same time." Alexandria began to feel all her emotions flare up, and she got goose bumps on her arms and a warm sensation in her cheeks.

"Why do you feel scared?" he asked.

Alexandria took a deep breath and very slowly let it out. As she began to speak her voice began to shake. "Because if he really is with someone else, that means that it's really over between us."

"But I thought you weren't together anymore?" He asked to sober her up and get her to move past what she wanted and see what the reality was. "What do you mean by 'really over'?"

"We aren't together. But that's not my choice; I still want to be with him." Alexandria said, understanding the reality but refusing to let go of her hopes and dreams.

"But if he's moved on, doesn't that mean that he doesn't want to be with you?"

"No. He's forcing himself to move on. But Dr. Robinson, I really believe he meant it when he said he loved me," she said. She refused what was and believed in her heart that if she remained faithful to him, things would change. She thought to herself, *if he tells me that it is over, I promise I will move on.*

She got the idea, in that moment, that she was going to call Landon.

After her session with Dr. Robinson ended, she hurried home. She had finally gotten her car back, but her parents were still monitoring her. When she arrived home, she picked up the house phone and dialed Landon's cell phone. There was no response, so she left a message.

"Hey, Landon. It's Alex. I know it's been awhile; I just wanted to check in on you and see how your summer was going. Call me back on my cell when you get a chance."

***

Alexandria didn't hear back from Landon and was becoming very anxious, so the next morning she decided she would stop by his new job on her way to cheerleading practice.

She had butterflies in her stomach as she pulled up because she didn't know what to expect. She didn't know if he was ignoring her or just didn't get the message, but she did need her answers. Alexandria walked into the retail store and asked the lady at the cash register if Landon was working. The older lady told her that he was stocking shelves towards the back. Alexandria started in the direction that the cashier was pointing. As she got closer, she tried to swallow but her mouth was completely dry. Just as she was about to turn back around because she hadn't planned what she was going to say, Landon saw her.

She blurted out, "Hey, Landon!" and she flashed a smile.

"Alex? What are you doing here?" he said surprised.

"Oh, I tried calling you. I heard you were working here now, so I wanted to stop by and see you," she said.

"Oh," he responded. He seemed bothered that she was there and he kept working.

"Hey," she said trying to gain his attention. She had questions, and she knew she could only get the answers from him. She went further "Are you with Brandi now?" She couldn't help it - she just had to know. If he was going to ignore her, she needed to know why.

"Yea, we're talking," He responded, "Is that what you came here to find out?"

"Yea. I mean, you seem like you're pissed at me. Like I did something wrong." She began to feel every emotional vein in her body flare up, and her eyes began to water.

"Look, I'm at work. We can talk about this some other time," he told her. Once he said that, he immediately regretted it.

"Ok. Will you call me tonight then?" Alexandria said with a sense of hopefulness. She knew that if he would call her, then there was still the possibility to work out whatever was messed up.

"Yea," he said hesitantly.

"Ok," she replied.

Alexandria proceeded to leave the store. She was indeed angry to hear about the new budding relationship; however, she ignored that thought and focused on the fact that they would talk later on that night.

The rest of the day, Alexandria prepped herself for the talk that she would have with Landon.

***

The conversation was nothing like she thought it would be. He did call her, and told her in a short two-minute monologue that he did love her and that he wasn't trying to hurt her, but he had to respect the wishes of her parents and his mother. He told her that it was best if they just moved on.

Alexandria couldn't comprehend how it could all be over so quickly. It had only been two years of her life, but it seemed like forever. How could he live happily ever after moving on so quickly? Did he not have feelings?

She decided that she would take a break from going to see Dr. Robinson for a while, but he still gave her phone check-ins once a week.

Things at home were much better, but they weren't completely back to normal. When Alexandria wasn't at cheer practice, Alexandria spent time with Liz, helping her at her hair salon in order to escape the walls of her bedroom.

***

Before the school year started, Liz decided that she would treat Alexandria to a shopping spree to kick off her senior year.

"Alex," Liz said, "Are you ready for your last year in high school?"

"I guess," she responded.

"I want you to know that sometimes, I know it can be difficult for you to talk to your mom. Trust me I know, she's my big sister. But you're my niece, and if you ever need anything, let me know. I love you and I'm here for you. Ok?"

"Thanks, Auntie - I love you too," she responded.

***

Alexandria was very nervous about the start of her senior year. She had new outfits and she looked and felt better than ever. She was in her room watching T.V. when the phone rang.

"Hello," she answered.

"Hi, Ms. Alexandria. How are you?" said the voice on the other end of the phone.

"I'm good, Dr. Robinson. I'm sorry I haven't been answering lately, but I've been doing much better," she assured him.

"Yes, I was able to talk to your mom. She told me that she sees progress, so it was ok if we go ahead and end our sessions. But I wanted to give you one last call."

"Thanks, Doc!"

"Are you feeling good about the upcoming school year?" he asked.

"Yes, sir."

"How do you feel about seeing Landon?"

"I'm nervous, but I know I can handle it. We actually spoke, and we both made the decision to move on," she informed him.

"Really?"

"Yea, so I am doing that."

"Well, I think it's a good decision. I just want to encourage you to stay focused. You have a bright future ahead of you, and you are much stronger than you think."

"Thanks, Dr. Robinson," she said smiling.

"You're welcome! And remember, I am only one phone call away."

"Yes, sir."

"Bye now."

"Bye."

CHAPTER 10

Alexandria decided that she would hang out with some friends so she called Kimberly.

"Hey, girl! Whatcha doing?" Kimberly asked.

"Nothing really. I'm just looking for something to do."

"Well, I'm at home bored as hell, honey. You can come over if you like."

"Cool. I can be there in about 30 minutes."

When Alexandria arrived, Kimberly's best friend Camille was there as well.

"Hey, Kim. Hey, Camille. I didn't know you would be here."

"Oh, yea girl, I just got off work. Got here maybe like 10 minutes ago... I just can't believe y'all are about to be seniors!!?"

"Yea! I'm so ready! All my shopping is done. Just ready for this year to be over with."

Camille was in the 10th grade, but she and Kimberly had been best friends for years.

"So, what are you ladies trying to get into?" asked Kimberly.

"I mean I'm down for whatever," Alexandria responded.

"Lex, how's Landon?" Camille asked.

"Oh, I guess he's fine. We had to break up because my parents thought we were getting too close and I needed to focus on school," Alexandria said.

"That's messed up," Camille said, "Y'all were so cute together!"

"Thanks..."

"You didn't get pregnant did you?" Camille quizzed while laughing hysterically.

"No. Absolutely not!"

"Good," she said still chuckling.

"So, what all have you two been doing all summer?" Alexandria asked them.

"Lex, it's been a crazy summer, but I knew your mom had you on lockdown," Kimberly said.

"Yea girl, I turned stalker-ish for a minute, but I'm back to normal now," Alexandria said laughing.

"You dodged some bullets by your distraction, so that's good," said Kimberly.

"What does that mean?" Alexandria asked, confused.

Kimberly looked at Camille then replied, "We were just wild'in out. You know? Just going to party after party since the new year came in."

"You guys stay at a party!" Alexandria laughed.

Whenever they did talk, Kimberly was always telling Alexandria about a new teen club she heard of or went to.

"I know, right?" Kimberly chuckled. "Well, towards the end of the school year, maybe like around April, I found out I was pregnant, and then literally two months later, Cam found out she was pregnant."

"WHAT?!?!"

"Yesss, girl!"

"Oh my gosh! What did you do? Better yet, what did your mom do, Kim?"

"Are you crazy, Lex? I didn't tell her... Camille found this clinic that one of the girls she goes to school with went to. I just asked my dad for some money and got an abortion."

"Are you serious?"

"Yea, we both did. I mean of course I don't feel great about it, but I had to do what I had to do."

"Wow, Kim. That sounds really intense."

"Yea it was. But now we're both on birth control."

"Wow. I mean, I'm on birth control too, but I'm not having sex...any more that is."

"Then what's the point of being on it?" asked Camille.

"I don't know. Just in case I ever do," Alexandria responded with a chuckle.

Alexandria was less experienced in the sexual department than them. They had been with multiple partners, and she couldn't even get over the one she had broken up with a little over 6 months ago.

Kimberly was looking through her phone when a text message came in and then said, "Y'all want to go to a cookout? One of the guys I know is hosting it and he just invited us?"

"You know I'm down; I ain't doing shit else anyways," said Camille.

"Yea, sure. I guess." Alexandria said hesitantly.

Camille looked at Alexandria and said, "Girl, you can't go into your senior year feeling sorry for yourself about that asshole."

"Camille, what are you talking about?" Kimberly snapped. "Alex," she continued, "I love you, and I know you had a lot going on this summer, so I didn't want to say anything."

"What are you guys talking about?" Alexandria said as she let out a sigh.

"Landon and I had school together this summer."

"Really?"

"Yea, girl. He told me that your parents didn't want him talking to you anymore when I confronted him about this girl he was trying to get with in our class."

"Was her name, Brandi?" Alexandria asked.

"Nah, it wasn't Brandi."

"Oh, because he's with a girl named Brandi now."

"Hold up," Camille interjected, putting up her hands. "I knew about the breakup, but I at least thought you guys

He'S A GOOD GUY, JUST NOT YOURS

would work that shit out. Didn't he get you a promise ring or something like that?"

"He did. But, no - he said it's just better if we both try and move on."

Kimberly said, "I asked him if he was going to work it out with you once things cooled down, but he basically blew off the question like what's the point? He told me that too much had happened, and he didn't want to deal with all the extra drama that the relationship came with. I told him that was harsh because it was never an issue before, you know? But then he said your mom and dad went to his house and pretty much made him out to be this bad guy in front of his parents. Telling them about how you lost your virginity in a bad way."

"I had to tell my mom what happened. There was no getting around it," Alexandria said in her defense.

"He said you told her all the details."

"Well, yea. But I wasn't trying to make him look bad. I mean my parents were pissed off. I'm their teenage daughter!"

"Well, that's what he thinks you did. But he said that he loved you, but it just had to be that way."

"Well, I definitely don't get that."

Alexandria was confused. She thought, *if Landon really loved her like he'd told Kimberly, then why couldn't they just work it out?*

"I don't know, girl. He was just really over it."

Alexandria didn't know what to say. A million questions and thoughts began to flood her mind; she thought she was going to burst into tears right there. Then her phone rang.

"Hey, Steven."

"Hey, Alex. What are you up to?"

"I'm just hanging out with Kim and her friend Camille." Alexandria and Steven had begun to talk a little more over the summer, and they were finally at a good place.

"I just wanted to call and check-in on you. I know school is about to start in a couple of days, this being your senior year and all."

"Yea. I'm pretty stoked about it!"

"That's good. You should be...I know you're with your friends, but I just wanted to call you. So, what are y'all doing?"

"I think we're about to go to a cookout."

"Ok. Well, if I don't talk to you before school starts, stay focused and start this year making great memories. You're a beautiful girl with a bright future. And remember, you don't have to do anything you don't want to do. The decisions that you make today will impact the rest of your life."

"Yea, I know…"

"Ok. Well, I'll talk to you later, and be safe."

"I will. Bye!"

As soon as Alexandria got off the phone, Kimberly faced her. "You seem irritated."

"Yea, he calls with encouragement, but things haven't really been the same since he moved out and got his girlfriend. I don't even like her. No one does."

"Damn, Lex, what'd she do to you? Let your brother live. At least he calls."

"Yea, I guess. But just like he feels I could do better – I believe he can too."

"Of course you do, he's your brother," Camille joked.

They all laughed and then Kimberly headed upstairs to get ready.

***

When they arrived, there were so many people there, but it seemed they were already packing up to leave.

Kimberly yelled from the car window, "Party over??"

One of the guys from the party about to get into his car responded, "Nah, we just taking it to the crib."

As he finished his statement, Kimberly had spotted a friend whom she flagged down to come over to the car. When he got to the car, Kimberly quizzed, "What's going on? You weren't going to tell me that you were moving the party?"

"Nah baby, it's not that we're just limited in space and activity here in this park. People just keep showin' up, so I'm taking it to the house. I was gonna text you though."

"Whatever. So, who we following? You?" Kimberly asked.

"Yea, I'm over there," he said as he pointed to his car. "We're about to head out now."

He ran back to his car and Alexandria, who was driving, followed him. "Kim, how old is this guy?" she asked.

"Don't trip, Alex. He's 31 but he's chill and he got money. Plus, it's not even serious."

"Well, duh! I hope not – you're not even 18 yet!"

"Don't you think I know how old I am? We just hang out, that's all. At his parties, everyone be here. So loosen up and puh-lease allow someone to entertain you!"

"I know I will. I see a cutie already," Camille said snapping her fingers in the air as she pretended to dance in the back seat. "I just hope he ain't come to the beach with sand," she giggled.

Alexandria didn't want to loosen up. She didn't even want to be at the party, but she needed to get her mind off Landon before she went back to school. She made up in her mind that whatever happened and whoever she met from that moment on, she wanted to meet.

When they arrived and went into the house, they all followed Kimberly to meet her friend. Kimberly greeted him with a hug and a kiss and said, "Baby, I want you to meet my friends Camille, who you already met once before, and this is my girl, Alex." Then Kimberly turned to her friends and said, "Ladies, this is Rodney." They all greeted one another with handshakes, and Kimberly then whispered in Rodney's ear, and he motioned to one of his friends to come over.

"Jay. These ladies here are VIP guests. Show them around and make sure they're comfortable, you got me?"

Rodney said.

"I got you. Ladies, follow me."

***

Alexandria was actually able to get her mind off the issues that she would have to face once school started. She and the girls had gone their separate ways, and she was still hanging out with Jay.

"So, are you having a good time?" he asked her.

"Yea, aside from the fact my friends totally deserted me," she snickered. "I'm having a blast!"

"I know it's kinda loud in here. You wanna go somewhere more quiet?" he asked.

"I guess."

She wasn't in the mood to be around everyone at the party anymore, and Jay was a pretty nice guy. She didn't see anything wrong with talking to him. Jay led her upstairs into a bedroom and closed the door.

"Whose room is this?"

"Oh, it's mine," Jay replied.

"You live here?"

"Yea, we're all roommates."

"So, it's like eventful every night, huh?"

"What you mean by eventful?" he said laughing.

"Parties...girls... you know what I'm talking about."

"Girl, chill. We not even like that," he laughed.

"How old are you?" she asked.

"Twenty-three."

"What are you doing hanging out with a 31-year-old man?"

"Dammmn - he's my cousin. Not blood, but we grew up together. He relocated here a couple of years ago, and after college, I was having a problem finding a job back home; but he found me something here, so I moved down."

"Oh."

"Feel bad?"

"No, not really," Alexandria giggled. "Look, I'm 17. I think it's only fair you know."

"Why? You think imma try and have sex with you?"

"I don't really know you all that well to answer that question."

"Well, I'm not. I'm a little buzzed, and you sexy as hell - but I can tell you ain't with all that. You didn't even take one hit or sip of nothing. So I know this ain't your scene anyways." He laughed.

"Oh, so you think you got me figured out, huh? I have you know; I'm driving for one – and for two, I don't smoke."

"Hummm, and three, you probably got a boyfriend."

"Negative."

Jay turned his TV on. "Anything you want to watch? You know your girls ain't going to be ready for at least another two hours," he joked. "That's enough time for you to watch a good movie. You can stay up here if you want."

She looked at him and mockingly said, "Oh, so now you're tired of babysitting me. Is that it?"

"Nah, I would have locked you in here a long time ago if that was the case. Half the party gone, I just gotta get up for work in the morning, and I was gonna catch some zz's."

"You know what, I think I'm just going to let you get your sleep, and I'll go back out to the party."

"Is that what you really want? I mean you did come up here."

"Well, I thought we were gonna talk…"

"So, you wanna talk to me," he smiled at her. "About

what?"

"Nothing. I'm going to just leave now."

Jay was standing closer to the door. As she walked by him, he grabbed her waist. "Don't go."

Alexandria stood there, feeling empty and at the same time, feeling wanted. She didn't know what to do. She didn't feel the same way she felt when Landon touched her. She didn't feel anything. But she didn't want him to think that she was just a little girl playing around. She followed him into the room because she did want to talk to him. He was showing her attention even if all he wanted to do was sleep. But she didn't want to leave and not try to move pass Landon. So, she kissed him, and he kissed her back.

They stood by the door passionlessly kissing one another. Then he began to unbuckle her belt, and she stopped kissing him and walked towards on the bed. No one said anything. Jay followed her and continued to kiss her. Alexandria pulled off her shorts, and began touching her as he pulled her panties to the side. Jay placed his fingers inside of her. He moved his fingers back and forth, and she felt her body responding. She was getting very moist. As he continued kissing her neck and filling her breast, something different happened, she felt a release that she never felt before. She couldn't believe it – she had an orgasm on a guy she didn't even love. *What was going on?* She wondered. She stopped kissing him, and all she could do was moan and curl up into a tiny ball.

"You ok?" he asked gently.

"Yea. I'm sorry but I need to use your bathroom."

Her panties were wet, and she needed to clean off. Jay showed her to the bathroom, and she quickly cleaned herself up and came back to the room. Jay was standing near the bed and asked, "You sure you're ok?"

"Yea, you're not mad are you?"

"At what? That it felt good to you? Hell nah - that's the loosest you been all night! I feel accomplished."

Buzz! Buzz!

Alexandria's phone vibrated because of an incoming text.

KIM:	Where are you?
ALEX:	I'm here. Ready to go?
KIM:	Yea, we're outside
ALEX:	Coming!

She looked at Jay and said, "I'm sorry, but I gotta go - the girls are ready."

"Well, what's your number? Maybe we can hang out."

"Where's your phone?" she asked.

Alexandria typed her number into his phone, and she walked herself outside.

Kimberly said, "GIRRLLL, YOU GOT SOME EXPLAINING TO DO! RUNNING OFF WITH THAT GUY!"

"Shut up, Kim!" Alexandria yelled, "Nothing happened."

"Suuurre," Kimberly said as she shot her friend a smile.

CHAPTER 11

School finally started, and Jay and Alexandria kept in touch with each other over the phone even though they hadn't seen each other again.

Alexandria managed to dodge Landon in the halls. It was pretty easy because they had no classes together. She did however hear about Landon daily. Most of her friends were pretty upset over the breakup and seeing Landon move on. All of her teammates that had classes with him kept telling her how they told him how stupid he was.

Alexandria took a hall pass in the middle of class one day to use the restroom. As she walked down the hall, the double doors opened from outside and in walked Landon. No one else was in the hall, and she always thought that if she ever did see him in school, she would melt, but that didn't happen. For some reason she was calm - he walked right by her and didn't say anything. Then she turned around and yelled, "Hey, Landon!" but he kept walking.

The days for Alexandria were pretty normal. She stayed busy with cheerleading for her high school and a local gym's All-Star competitive team that she'd joined and of course schoolwork itself. She thought about Landon often, but all she really felt was sorry for herself. She thought that after he saw her, he would at least want to talk to her. But that hope was fading away. She felt completely dogged out.

***

It was a Friday afternoon; the day of the homecoming pep rally, and all the seniors would meet in the senior hallway afterwards as tradition before the game. Alexandria was standing with all the cheerleaders and football players, and as the rally was closing and the students were going their separate ways, she spotted Landon in the crowd. He was standing there with his arm around Brandi's neck, and her arm was wrapped around his waist. He didn't see Alexandria looking at them as he kissed his new girlfriend on the lips.

Every emotion that Alexandria was trying to keep under control came rushing through her veins, and Alexandria burst into tears.

"What's wrong, Lex?!?" All of her friends around began to ask, but it was an uncontrollable firework of water.

Landon had parted ways with Brandi and just so happened to be walking in Alexandria's direction. He saw everyone around her and pushed through the crowd, getting face to face with Alexandria and said, "Are you ok? What's wrong, what happened??"

All the anger that was inside Alexandria came raging out, and she screamed, "GET AWAY FROM ME!!"

Landon was concerned when he stopped, but at that moment, he regretted it since everyone stood staring at him. He stood there, looking at the tears streaming down the face of the girl that he loved. He didn't understand how it all changed, and he was trying his best to move on. But he couldn't stand to know that the tears pouring down her face could be because of him.

One of the counselors, Ms. Bates, that was in the hallway ran over and cleared the hall and moved Alexandria into the office. When Ms. Bates finally calmed Alexandria down, she asked her what was wrong. Alexandria didn't want to talk to her - she didn't want to talk to anyone. Ms. Bates then said, "Look, whatever it is sweetie, it's going to be okay." Most of the community knew Alexandria because of her involvement in sports. They supported her, but at the moment, even while being known, she still felt alone.

"Are you going to be okay?" Ms. Bates asked.

"Yes ma'am," Alexandria managed to get out.

Alexandria stayed in her office until it was time to go to the game. She pulled her emotions together and made it through the night.

After the game, Alexandria saw a text from Landon:

LANDON: Hey Alex, I'm sorry. So much is going on. I know you're mad at me, but I want to talk to you. Can I call you?

She noticed the text was sent during the game, but she immediately responded.

ALEX: Are you up?

Five minutes later Alexandra received an incoming call.

Ring! Ring! Ring!

"Hello," Alexandria said.

"Hey," answered the voice at the other end of the phone.

"Hey, Landon."

"Lex. I miss you so much."

Alexandria had been waiting for Landon to say that. She was trying so hard to be cool with everything before her break down, but it seemed to help her situation with

Landon, his seeing her distressed. She didn't want to keep going through hoops to pretend she didn't care.

"Then why are you with her?" she shot back at him.

"Alex. I needed a way to move on - she's not a bad girl."

"Do you love her?"

"No. Alex, you know I still love you."

"Then why are you with her?" she asked again.

"Alex, it's not that simple. I thought you'd moved on."

"How could you possibly think that, Landon?"

"You walk around school now like it doesn't bother you. I've been wanting to reach out to you. I just didn't know what you would do, and everyone keeps giving me a hard time about the whole situation. This is really hard."

"Why is it so hard for you, you miss me, you love me… so, I don't get it."

"I can't just tell her now; I don't want to be with you. That wouldn't be right."

"You should have never told her you wanted to be with her," Alexandria stated with tears forming in her eyes.

"Look, I want to see you. Can you come over tomorrow?"

Alexandria felt butterflies in her stomach. She was excited and nervous all at the same time. "Yea, what time?"

"Well, my mom is out of town so whenever you can."

"Ok."

"I love you," he said.

"I love you too," she responded.

After they hung up the phone, Alexandria quickly got ready for bed in high hopes of the next day.

The next morning, there was a knock on her bedroom door.

"Come in," Alexandria said. It was Ms. Anderson.

"Hey, I wanted to let you know that I called Dr. Robinson and told him what happened yesterday at school. He wants you to give him a call."

"Ok." Alexandria responded, "I will." She continued "Mom - do you think it would be ok if I stayed the night at Kim's?"

"Do you think that it's a good time?"

"Yea. I just want to get my mind off of things, and she always helps."

"I guess that will be ok. You have to be back tomorrow before dinner."

"Ok, I will."

Alexandria had no intentions of going over to Kimberly's house; she just needed a way to spend the night with Landon just in case everything went well. She packed a bag and headed over to his house. On her way out, she thought to herself that she would need to park in the garage since her Aunt and Landon stayed in the same subdivision.

She gave Landon a call to leave the garage open so she could hide her car in there. Then she remembered that she was supposed to call Dr. Robinson. When she finally arrived at Landon's house, she pulled into the garage and stayed in her car to get the call out of the way.

"Hello, Ms. Alexandria, I'm glad you called."

"Hey, Dr. Robinson."

"How are you feeling today?"

"Everything is better now. Yesterday was a rough day. The first one in a long time."

"I heard. I'm glad you're feeling better. What happened?"

"Really, it was the first time that I saw Landon and his new girlfriend together, and they kissed."

"Ouch. I know that must have been difficult."

"Yea, it was. But he called me, and we talked about it. Pretty much made everything much better because he was finally honest and told me that he loved and missed me."

"Really? While he's still with the new girl?"

"Yea. But he's going to break up with her."

"Alex, I'm here for you. And you know that I would never tell you what to do. I'm not speaking as a professional when I say this, but as a close friend of your family and someone that cares about you very much. Alex, dear, whatever you do, don't have sex with Landon..." Dr. Robinson continued speaking, but his words kept ringing in her ear...*Don't have sex with Landon.*

After the conversation had ended, Alexandria headed for the door, and Landon was standing there waiting on her. He greeted her with a big hug that got her up off her feet, and he spun her around. "I'm glad you came!"

"I told you I would."

After he stopped, she adamantly went to the living room.

"Listen Landon. If we are going to be together, you have to break up with her."

"I was going to tell you last night, but I decided to wait and tell you face to face. I broke up with Brandi yesterday, and Alex, I know now that I want to be with you."

"You did it already! How?"

"Last night, I went over there, and we talked. I told her that I couldn't do it anymore."

"What did she say?"

"She cried a little, but she knows I still love you."

"I got your text right after it happened so I called you as soon as I got in the car."

"Landon. You do know that we have to wait a while before we can be together, right?"

"Why?"

"Because you just got out of a relationship. That is so rude."

"Alex, I didn't think that we would talk again and now you are here. I don't care what people think."

"Well, I don't either. But I do know that when you like someone, and you break up, it's not easy seeing them with another person - let alone the very next day. That's not cool."

"Ok, but I don't care."

"I do."

"Ok - whatever you want. I'm just glad you are here."

Landon sat on the couch and motioned for Alexandria to sit next to him. Once she did, he began to kiss her.

"Landon, slow down. We have a lot to talk about."

"Alex, you don't want to be seen with me right now or whatever, but no one is here. No one can see us...I miss you."

"Babe, I miss you too. I want you. But I still have questions that need answers."

Landon wanted to make sure that the relationship between him and Alexandria hadn't changed. But every time he tried to get close to her, she would stop him.

She replayed Dr. Robinson's advice to not have sex with Landon. Landon whispered in her ear, "You will always be mine."

"Alex, isn't this what you want? I don't get it. Why do you keep stopping me?"

Alexandria didn't know how to respond. A part of her wanted things with Landon to go back to the way they were, but then another part of her wanted to know what had happened in his previous relationship. She didn't want to push him away, but she didn't want the feeling of not being wanted. She felt so confused. When he finally chosen to be with her, all she could think about was why he left.

"Alex, I love you."

Those words sounded so good to her. As he said it, all her worries just seemed to disappear, and she leaned over and began to kiss him.

Landon stopped and looked into her eyes and said, "I will never leave you. Remember, I'll always come back to you... and I'm sorry for hurting you."

With tears in her eyes, she gave in and allowed Landon back into her life. As they rekindled the passion of their relationship on the living room couch. "You will always be mine," he told her.

***

When Alexandria arrived Monday at school, rumors started to go around that Brandi and Landon had broken up. One of Alexandria's friends from the cheerleading team quizzed her with excitement. "So are you all going to get back together?"

"I don't know, I hope so," Alexandria responded.

"I mean why else would he break up with her? Alex, you know Landon loves you. I just knew you two would get back together!"

Alexandria was filled with so much joy on the inside. *At least, people are expecting us to get back together*, she thought.

"Hey Alex," Gia said rushing over to the lunch table where Alexandria was sitting. They hadn't spoken much since their girl's day at the pool. "So, you heard the news about Landon and Brandi, right?"

"Yea, I know. Everyone has been telling me."

"I hope you are not planning on getting back together with him?"

"Why not? You do know that this is a dream come true. He finally broke up with her!" She didn't understand why her friend wasn't happy for her. "What's your problem? I thought you liked Landon?" she asked Gia, puzzled.

"Are you serious right now Alex! He's a f'ing loser! I didn't like them together, but I definitely don't like that he broke up with her right after he had sex with her!"

Alexandria's heart sank into her stomach. "What? Where did you hear that?"

"You didn't know that?" Gia asked. "That's what she's telling everyone, and I don't believe that she's lying about it."

Alexandria was speechless. She didn't know what to say. "You mean they had sex?"

"I mean, that loser slept with her and then got up, put his clothes on and then said *oh, by the way, I don't want to be with you anymore.*"

"I don't believe you."

"Believe what you want, Lex."

Alexandria couldn't believe it. She didn't want to believe it. She felt sick to her stomach. She got up from the lunch table and walked outside. She called her mom.

"Mom, I don't feel so good."

"What's wrong?"

"I don't know; I just feel sick. I think I need to come home."

"Alex, are you sure you can't just wait it out? School is over in 2 hours."

"No, mom, I want to come home now."

"Ok."

Alexandria went to the attendance office so that her mom could check her out. After she left the office, she ran to her car and cried. She didn't understand how she could go from being the happiest girl on the earth to feeling like the worst.

She stayed in her room for the remainder of the day. Around 3 o'clock, she received a call from Landon.

"Hey Babe, I heard you left school early; are you ok?"

"Landon. Please tell me it isn't true!"

"Tell you what's not true?" he asked clueless.

"Did you have sex with that girl?"

"What do you mean, where did you hear that?"

"LANDON, DID YOU HAVE SEX WITH HER AND THEN BREAK UP WITH HER?" her voice rising.

"Alex, where is this coming from?"

"LANDON, PLEASE JUST ANSWER THE QUESTION!" Alexandria sternly said with tears running down her face.

Landon didn't know what to say. He wanted to be with Alexandria, but if he answered the question, he knew it would be over. "Alex, we weren't together."

"So you did?" she asked calming down.

"Alex!"

"Landon...Please just answer the question," she said again. "Did you or did you not have sex with Brandi?"

"Yes, I had sex with her."

Alexandria couldn't take it. She couldn't believe it. She didn't know what to think. She didn't know what to say. "I HATE YOU!!" she shouted and dropped the phone.

CHAPTER 12

Alexandria decided that she couldn't be with Landon - at least not anytime soon, but Landon continued to pursue Alexandria. He couldn't have her leave him. The reason he broke up with Brandi in the first place was to be with her and now she wanted nothing to do with him.

Landon sent flowers to Mrs. Anderson to make things between them right. Until one day, he decided to go over and have a talk with her face to face. He apologized to her for what happened before the summer, and he asked her if he could see Alexandria again. Once he was in good graces with Mrs. Anderson. He needed to make things right with Alexandria.

***

It had been about a week and a half and Landon noticed something was wrong, and so he went to the doctor. Later on that day at school, he approached Alexandria because she hadn't been answering any of his phone calls.

"What the hell is wrong with you? Why aren't you answering any of my calls?"

"Well, that's an easy one asshole, because I don't want to talk to you!"

"You fucking hoe!"

"Oh, I'm the hoe now?! How dare you talk to me like that? Get the hell away from me." She spewed trying to force herself away from him

"Don't" worry; I will stay far away from you. Just make sure you go get yourself checked. Gonorrhea isn't something you want to ignore."

As Landon stormed away, all Alexandria could think was *this just keeps getting worse*. She couldn't focus at school, she couldn't focus after school, and now she had to deal with this.

Gradually, after Whitley and Alexandria's relationship dwindled down, she started talking more to Kimberly. She immediately called her.

"Kim!"

"Hey, girl. What's up?"

"I need your help. I need to get to a clinic. Do you know any?"

"Everything alright?"

"Yea, it's Landon. He has gonorrhea, and we messed around, and I just want to be sure I don't have it."

"Let me look up something, and I will text you."

"Thanks!"

Rumors began to surface that Landon was going around calling Alexandria a hoe. Gia had a class with Alexandria and asked her what was going on.

"I don't know girl. The kid is crazy," Alexandria answered.

"He's like pissed at you."

"He thinks I slept with someone else."

"Well, why does it matter to him? I thought you guys were over."

"Well, we are. But we were talking."

Gia rolled her eyes. "Ok, and so what if you did? He slept with someone else too."

"I know."

On cue Alexandria's phone buzzed with an incoming text. It was from Kimberly with the information to the clinic. Alexandria decided that she had to go to the clinic that day.

She couldn't tell anyone that she was going because she didn't know how she would explain it. She drove all the way to the clinic after school and got there to realize that it was closed. They only opened during the hours that she was in school. Alexandria sat in her car and cried, but her tears were interrupted by the ringing of her phone.

"Hello."

"Alex, where are you?"

"I'm on my way home."

"Alex, this is out of control! Your coach called and said that you missed practice. Where did you go?"

"Mom. I said I'm on my way home," Alexandria repeated; then she hung up the phone.

Alexandria was so angry. It seemed like the walls were closing in on her everywhere she turned. When she got home, her mom and dad were at the kitchen table.

"Alex, sit down and let's talk," her dad said.

Alexandria walked into the kitchen and sat at the table. She was unbothered with whatever her parents had to say.

"Alex, this cannot go on. You come home, and you don't say anything. You don't talk to us, you don't talk to your brother, and you don't talk to Dr. Robinson. We're concerned with your behavior; it isn't normal. "What's" wrong?" her dad asked.

"Nothing."

"Why did you miss practice today?"

"Because I had something to do," Alexandria responded rolling her eyes.

Mrs. Anderson tried to understand her daughter's emotions but she had it with Alexandria's disrespect. She interrupted and said, "I will not tolerate this behavior in my home. None of your other brothers and sisters gave us this much trouble. If you think you are grown and you don't have to talk to us, then you can get out!" you could hear the disappointment in her tone as she continued.

"Your grades are horrible. Your school and teachers are calling left and right. I can't continue to do this. We've tried to get you help, and you don't want it. And then we ask you where you are, and you hang up the phone with no explanation. You're driving the car that we bought, so I want my keys back now!"

Alexandria threw the keys on the table. "Here you go mom, does this answer your questions?"

"You're also using the phone that we pay the bill for, so I would like that back as well."

Alexandria slammed the phone on the table. "Are we done?" She felt so alone, and she wanted to scream.

"I don't know where I went wrong Alex; please tell me," her mother pleaded.

"I need a ride to the clinic tomorrow morning. Can one of you take me?" Alexandria asked.

"Why do you need a ride to the clinic?" her mother responded.

"Because I might have gonorrhea, and I need to go get checked," she said, emotionless.

"Why would you have gonorrhea, Alex?" her mother asked. "Who did you get it from, Landon?"

"No, it's not Landon," Alexandria shot back.

"Who is it then?"

"I don't know."

"So you mean to tell me that you are just going around having sex with people you don't know?"

"No. I just don't know who it could be."

"Well, let's ask an easier question. Who all have you had sex with?"

"Mom, I just feel like I have something." Alexandria had read about the symptoms and she was beginning to feel like she had some of them.

"So, you're still not going to talk?"

"I've only had sex with three people. You don't know them, so it's pointless to tell you," Alexandria lied. She didn't want to say she only had sex with one person. The one person she wanted to be with – that she wasn't supposed to be with. She did not want to admit that same person was the one that possibly gave her an STD.

"I'm not taking you anywhere until you tell me who gave you an STD."

"Fine. I will just die then!" she said dramatically as she stormed upstairs.

Her mother chased after her and said, "Not in my house you won't. Pack your things and get out! Get out of my house!"

Alexandria began to pack her things and screamed at her parents. "Fine – I will leave! I don't care. Y'all don't love me anyways!"

Tears began to pour out as she threw all her clothes into trash bags. Her dad walked in and opened his arms toward Alexandria to give her a hug.

"Alex, we love you," he said as he embraced her.

"Daddy, I don't want to be here anymore," she said through the tears and shortness of breath.

She grabbed the bags that she could, her journal and walked out of the house. She had nowhere to go, but she just didn't want to be in that house, she didn't want to go to that school, she didn't want to know the people she knew. She sat on her bags outside the front door until she cried herself to sleep.

That night she had another dream. She woke up in the middle of the night sitting under the dark sky and wrote in her journal.

> *I was sleeping in my bed and snakes started to crawl on me, and I ran out of the room. I ran to my brother's room and hid under the bed. Then one of my cousins came in and got on top of me. He lifted my shirt and began to feel my chest, but when I looked down, I realized that I wasn't even old enough to have breasts. He began to kiss me. It felt like a first kiss; I think I might even love him. He protected me and wouldn't let any of my other cousins pick on me.*

She woke up to her dad standing over her. The morning had come. He told her to go inside so she could get cleaned up and he would take her to the clinic.

"Dad," she said, "I don't want to go back inside."

"Alright," he said. She began to put her things in the back of his car. She looked through the bags and found a clean outfit to wear. As she got into the car, her dad asked, "Are you hungry?"

"Yes," she responded.

He took her to get something to eat at Burger King, and she went into the restroom to clean up. After breakfast, he took her to the clinic. When they got there, Mrs. Anderson and Liz were waiting out front.

"Alex, would you like to stay with me?" Liz asked as she walked up to the passenger seat window.

"I guess," she responded.

Alexandria got out of the car, and Liz helped her put the bags into the car, which Mrs. Anderson and her had been waiting by.

"What time do you get out of practice?" Liz asked.

"5."

"Ok, you need to be at the gym for me to pick you up."

"Ok," Alexandria replied.

Liz got into her car and drove away.

Alexandria looked at her mom and then her dad.

"Alex, your mom is going to take you to school after y'all leave the clinic, ok?"

"Yes, sir."

Her dad left for work. Initially Alexandria was nervous about the whole thing, but she was relieved that her mom was with her. Her relief quickly turned into anxiety when the time came for them to ride in the car. The silence was so present, that speaking in that moment felt awkward. *I'll just turn on the radio,* Alexandria thought.

***

When Alexandria made it to school later that day, she didn't go to class but instead went to find Landon.

He was in a class with a teacher she knew, so she walked in and asked if she could speak to Landon. The teacher allowed Landon to come out.

"So, it turns out that I am not a hoe. Actually, it turns out that I don't have anything at all," Alexandria shot at him.

"Yea right."

She pulled out her test results to show him the results were negative.

"Unlike you, when I said I love you. I really meant it," Alexandria said.

"I waited an entire year for you."

"Well, I'm beginning to think that you should've waited much longer. You're nasty."

"Alex..."

"No, we're done here. I just wanted to tell you to your face."

Alexandria walked away from Landon. She walked away relieved. Relieved that she didn't have an STD. Relieved that she didn't break her promise. Relieved that he was wrong and she was right. Relieved that she could finally move on.

Landon ran up to Alexandria.

"Alex!"

"What do you want Landon? I've gotta get to class."

"I'm sorry."

"What exactly are you sorry for this time?"

"I'm sorry for hurting you."

CHAPTER 13

A few weeks had passed; Alexandria was still living with her Aunt Liz, and she missed home. She hadn't talked to her parents and she didn't want to.

"Alex. Don't you think this has gone on long enough?" Liz asked.

Alexandria looked at her as Liz continued.

"I think you should call your mom. Or do you just want to continue to sleep on my couch and pull clothes out of a trash bag? This is your senior year, and you're supposed to be having fun. You don't go anywhere or hang out with anyone."

"I don't understand what people want from me," Alexandria said. "Are you tired of having me here?" she asked.

"No. But I also don't want you to be on bad terms with your mom. You know she loves you."

"I'll talk to her. I'm just not ready now."

"Well, she said that you can have your phone back." Liz handed her the phone

"Really?"

"Yea, so when you're ready, make sure you use it to call her."

Alexandria wasn't ready to go home, but she had made a new friend that she wanted to talk to. She was a transfer student that Alexandria met in business class.

She dialed the number.

"Hello?" said her new friend Bonnie.

"Hey Bernadine!" she said happily.

"Oh no! Only one person calls me that, LEXI POOH, is that you?!"

"Hey girl!"

"Heeeyyyyy! You got service?!" Bonnie joked.

"Yea, my mom gave me back my phone."

"You're back home?"

"No. I got my phone, so I would be able to call her when I'm ready."

"Great - I'm coming to get you. Send me your address!!!"

When Bonnie got there, she went inside to meet Alexandria's aunt, Liz.

"Hello, Auntie!" Bonnie said.

"Hey."

"Auntie, this is Bonnie, a new girl from school," Alexandria introduced her new friend.

"I'm her new sister just like you are her new mommy," Bonnie said.

"I'm *not* her new mommy," Liz retorted.

"I'm just kidding. We're going to get some ice cream - I hope that's ok?"

"Oh o---"

Before Liz could get the words out of her mouth, Bonnie interrupted and said, "Did you want us to bring you back something?"

"No, I'm alright."

"Alright, come on Lexi Pooh. Let's hit the road" Bonnie said, tugging on Alexandria's arm.

"So where to, my love?" Bonnie asked as they got in the car.

"Somewhere far away" Alexandria replied.

"Great - that's the only place I know how to get to," she said laughing.

Alexandria immediately loved business class when she met Bonnie. They quickly became friends probably because it helped her create a new life.

They arrived at the park.

"I was meeting Will here. You're officially my third wheel," Bonnie said to Alexandria as they were getting out of the car. When they arrived to where Will was sitting, he looked at Alexandria and said, "Fancy seeing you here."

"You leave her alone," Bonnie snapped back.

"Why you ain't with my boy, Landon?"

They all went to the same school, and everyone pretty much knew what was going on.

"I just need my space."

"Imma hit him up so you can meet him here. I don't know why y'all so stubborn."

Will texted Landon at that moment. Then he said to Alexandria, "You both trying to be tough. Don't you love him?"

"I thought I loved him."

"So you don't love him?"

"Love is not something you just quickly get over," she replied.

"Exactly, y'all too young to be fighting feelings, just go with the flow."

"Well, the flow isn't actually us being together."

"Yea, that's because your momma jumped in. It was flowing, and then you both had to find ways around this brick wall. You just gotta get back in the flow. Life is too short. He's a good guy, you feel me? Situations may be messy, but he loves you. And quite honestly, I'm tired of hearing about you from him," he laughed.

Alexandria wasn't exactly thrilled about seeing Landon after what he put her through, and she wasn't thrilled about being Bonnie's third wheel, but she needed something to do in the meantime. When Landon finally showed up, she made up in her mind that she wasn't going to be angry, but she wasn't going to be nice either.

As they sat on the swings on the playground, Landon asked her, "How are you?"

"I'm great," Alexandria responded sarcastically.

"So, you don't wanna talk to me."

"Listen, I never asked you to come here. "

"Alex, you know I'm sorry. I don't know what else you want me to say."

"I think you've said enough," she said as she got up and walked away. She didn't want to be mad, but she didn't want to pretend either.

Landon quickly chased after Alexandria and grabbed her by the arms and said. "Alex, stop it."

"Let me go," she said as she tried to remove herself from his grip.

He didn't let go.

"I love you. Why can't you see that?"

"Because you ruined everything, Landon! How could you have sex with her?"

"Alex. It meant nothing."

"Well, I guess you know now that a moment of nothing could cost you everything."

"I still love you," Landon said. Still holding her, he pulled her into his arms and said, "Baby, I'm sorry. I'm so sorry."

Landon wanted to be with Alexandria. He really cared about her and the way she felt. She was the first girl that actually had substance, she had goals and dreams, everyone loved her, she came from a nice family, and he wanted to be a part of all that. He loved her. He truly meant what he said when they first had sex, but things got blurred. He got caught up in a bad situation.

"I got caught up, Babe," he began to cry, "I really love you."

Alexandria had tears rolling down her face. When she was finally able to control all of her emotions, she looked directly into Landon's eyes and asked, "Then why would you have sex with her?"

***

Alexandria moved back home. Cheerleading season was over, and she was no longer interested in running track. She really wanted to work things out with Landon, but she wanted to take things slow. Alexandria told her mom everything – even about still wanting things with Landon to work out. After all that happened, Mrs. Anderson said that it was okay if he was the person she wanted to be with. She told Alexandria that she couldn't come crying to her if Landon hurt her again. Dr. Robinson also checked in with Alexandria from time to time.

One day during one of their check-ins he told her, "Alex, I feel as if there are some details in your past that you don't want to talk about."

"Doc, it's not that I don't want to talk about it; I just have a hard time remembering."

"You know, sometimes our mind will not bring up memories to protect us. I know you told me that you and Landon are back talking, but don't you want to understand what happened in the first place?"

"I do understand. He thought we would never get back together again so he moved on. I can't control that; all I can control is what happens next, and he wants to be with me."

"So, what happens if it doesn't work out?"

"Then we'll go our separate ways, Doc. But I can't worry about the unknown; I have to live in the now."

"I agree with living in the present, but you will have to deal with the past sooner or later, or it will deal with you." He continued, "Do you feel safe around Landon?"

"Yea, he loves me."

"Alex, love is not a moment. Your love for a person shouldn't be momentary or complimentary."

"We're just young now, but when we're older and married, we're going to defeat the odds, we're going to laugh at the past. He is my high school sweetheart, and I'm going to marry him."

"You know, before you said that you wanted to wait until marriage before having sex. What happened to that?"

Alexandria was quiet.

"Alex, I think that you should reconsider your goals. I don't think you should walk aimlessly. I think you should wait it out, and don't get back with Landon so soon because of a desire to prove people wrong or to fill a void."

"Who am I proving wrong?"

"I don't know, maybe you can answer that question?"

"So. I'm guessing that you're joining the bandwagon of me not being with Landon?"

"I'm looking out for your best interest."

"You don't even know me that well, Landon is my best friend. I tell him everything, and he loves me in spite of it all."

Deep down inside, Alexandria knew that Dr. Robinson was right. She knew it was too soon, but she also didn't see a reason to wait. It was her senior year, and if she didn't get things right with Landon before graduation, there was no telling what could happen.

A text came in and interrupted her thoughts.

LANDON: We need to talk.

ALEX: What's wrong?

LANDON: Call me.

***

Alexandria made the decision to get back with Landon, and they were just going to work through their issues together.

"She's what?!"

"She's pregnant," Landon replied sheepishly.

This was another thing that Alexandria had to take in. Brandi was claiming that she was pregnant.

Alexandria told him that she would be with him no matter what.

"I'm scared," Landon said.

"What are you gonna do?" Alexandria quizzed.

"I'm going to be there for my kid, but I don't want anything to do with Brandi."

Alexandria didn't have anyone that she could tell. She had pushed everyone away. Life at home was ok, but it wasn't the best. Her grades were ok, but they weren't the best. She wasn't focused on SAT and ACT scores, and she wanted to escape everything all together. Even her new friend Bonnie said that the entire situation was too much for a teenager to have to deal with. Alexandria was stressed out, and to top it all; she was experiencing irritation in her vagina.

"Mom?"

"What's wrong?"

"I think there's something wrong down there."

"What do you mean?"

"Can you take a look?"

Alexandria undressed herself and waited for Mrs. Anderson to look.

"Oh my goodness, Alex! This looks like warts!"

"What does that mean?"

***

The HPV/Genital Warts virus had become active in Alexandria. All the stress had triggered it, and for the second half of her senior year, Alexandria spent most of her time in the doctor's office.

"Where is Landon?" her mom asked.

"Mom, he has a lot going on right now."

Brandi decided to get an abortion, but the rift between Alexandria and Landon was still present. Landon felt bad that Alexandria had to go through it all; however, there was nothing he could do. Her STD made him question her loyalty. He had gotten checked for the HPV virus, but there was no trace. He began to accuse her of being with other people.

Graduation came and went, and high school was over. Landon stopped contacting Alexandria. After all of her treatments were over, Alexandria felt as though Landon abandoned her during the time she needed him the most. After all that had happened, Landon made the decision that he just needed time that summer to himself.

***

The entire summer they never spoke. It wasn't something that they both planned to do, Landon made the decision on his own. Alexandria spent the entire summer trying to move on, but it was difficult because she didn't understand why he didn't want to be with her. She became obsessed with talking about, thinking about, and knowing about Landon. It consumed her.

Alexandria didn't know where she would be going to school, but her heart was set on Valdosta State University. She found out towards the end of her senior year that she made the competitive cheerleading team, but she was still waiting on her ACT scores to be officially accepted.

She wanted to go to Valdosta because it was close to the school that Landon had been accepted into.

***

After weeks of waiting, Alexandria's scores came back.

By now, there were no room in the dorms, and housing for her would have to be an off-campus apartment.

Alexandria's parents said they would not be paying for the cost associated with going away and not staying on campus when there were more affordable schools around where she could commute from home. So much had been going on with Alexandria that her parents didn't feel comfortable letting her go away far.

It was hard for Alexandria to come to grips that she would not being going away to school because she hadn't been focused like she should have during high school. All the time apart from Landon gave her the clarity to see that she wasn't living the life that she knew she was capable of living. She made the decision that she would move on and begin to pick up the pieces.

CHAPTER 14

Alexandria was so relieved to be in college finally even though it was a community college. Honestly, it was the first in a long time that she felt like she was doing something right. It was a step in the right direction. It was different from high school, it was good to not be surrounded by the same friends that she grew up with her entire life. It was a new beginning.

Alexandria was so focused, and there were no distractions. To her, it felt like freshman year of high school. She knew deep down inside that this was her time to let go of everyone in the past, anything that reminded her of the past and just embrace her second chance at a bright future.

She did miss her friends, but almost everyone was away at college. The only person who stayed at home with Alexandria was Bonnie; however, she decided that she wanted to take a semester off. Alexandria knew that this was truly a great place for her to be in.

Alexandria and Landon had actually stopped talking over the summer. It was something that neither of them tried to fight. So much had happened. They both needed time and space to breathe. She took the time to take a step back and see the bigger picture. The distance between them actually made her see that there was an option to rebuild their relationship. Inside the relationship, all she ever saw was the smoke. All the problems they went through didn't seem as important.

Time was her biggest friend. Time gave Alexandria a chance to look past all the debris in her life and see that opportunity was still waiting on her.

***

School was great for Alexandria; she was actually enjoying her professors, and she was so engaged that she was the top student in two of her five classes. That was a huge accomplishment for her because for once; she was getting ahead. She was working at an amazing engineering firm and making decent money. She was still at home with her parents which helped with saving because she didn't have many bills to pay.

"Hey, mom," she said as she walked into the home office that Mrs. Anderson was working from.

"Yea, what's up?" she responded as she looked up from the paperwork she was going through.

"I know you're in the middle of something - "

"Oh, you're more important than this. Is everything ok?"

"Yea." Alexandria didn't really have anything to say; she just wanted to talk to her mom. She knew that the past couple of years had weighed on their relationship. She just felt the need to talk to her. Mrs. Anderson waited but then continued with another question, "How's school? Everything still going well?"

"Oh, yea. School is really great! I've even managed to meet a couple of people."

"I know it's not like going away, but whenever you want to hang out, just keep me and your dad in the loop."

"Of course. You know Steven and Drew are supposed to be taking me out in a few weeks." She couldn't wait to spend time with her older brothers. Steven and Alexandria weren't in such a close space, but they were in a good place. It seemed as though age was a part of the issue in Alexandria's and Steven's relationship. As she got older he started inviting her out with him more.

"Yea. Drew will be here for a couple of weeks. You know those boys party hard?"

"Yea, but this will be the first time that I've hung out with them together." Although it was Alexandria's first time hanging out as an adult with both her brothers, she was nervous, but she knew they would take good care of her.

"So, you really seem to be in a good place," Mrs. Anderson stated.

"Yea, I feel really good, mom."

"I'm proud of you, sweetheart."

Just then, Alexandria received a text.

LANDON: How r u

She was a little taken back to see Landon's name on her screen. Alexandria's expression alarmed Mrs. Anderson as she saw Alexandria look down at her phone.

"Is everything ok?" Mrs. Anderson asked.

Alexandria looked up, trying to act normal, but that didn't usually fly with her mom.

"Uh, yea. Just a text from Landon..." Alexandria hadn't told her mother that Landon and she had stopped talking. Alexandria led her to believe that the distance was helping their relationship.

"How's Landon?"

"Honestly, mom, we haven't spoken in a few months. I just got a text from him asking me how I'm doing." Alexandria knew Mrs. Anderson had her best interest at heart. Mrs. Anderson remained understanding even though Alexandria had been difficult.

"Alex, you know I love you, but what do you still see in him? Don't you get tired of going back and forth?"

Alexandria sat there thinking about her mom's questions, and the best way to answer them. She had thought about it before, but she knew that the best way for her to continue forward in life was to be honest. Even if people didn't appreciate her truth.

Then she responded, "You know what mom? I do get tired of going back and forth. But it's like something still hasn't *clicked* completely for me. I hear everything everyone says about Landon and our relationship, but I believe that if I move out and stop being a kid and Landon and I were to go through one of our episodes, I wouldn't want to go back with him. I would be an adult that didn't have time to play childish games."

Mrs. Anderson looked at Alexandria as she spoke. But Alexandria honestly felt that way. She still felt like a child, and she believed that when given the opportunity to be a man instead of a boy if Landon failed, her eyes would be open to it. But for now, she was comfortable with no responsibilities. She was okay with the emotional roller coaster, theme park relationship.

"I hope so," Mrs. Anderson responded.

Alexandria decided not to respond to Landon right away, but she was pretty excited that he reached out to her after all that time. She didn't want him to think that because he was thinking about her that she was thinking about him – even though she was.

**

Thanksgiving rolled around and a lot of Alexandria's friends and family members were in town, and this was the weekend that she would be hanging out with her brothers, Andrew and Steven. It was perfect because she had just turned 18, and she was now able to get into some of the clubs that they would be going to.

"TuTu!" Andrew, Alexandria's oldest brother, called her TuTu – she hated that nickname. Not only did it not make any sense, but no one called her that anymore. He barged into her room without knocking.

"My name is Alex or Alexandria..." she shot back, annoyed with his inability to knock. However, she knew that fighting back would start a war that she couldn't win.

"Excuse me, *A l e x a n d r i a*, what are you doing tonight?" Andrew asked as he plopped down on her bed.

"Nothing. Are we going out tonight? I thought it was tomorrow?" Alexandria was laying down after a long day of grocery shopping with Mrs. Anderson for Thanksgiving dinner.

"Yea, but I got somewhere special that I want to take you."

Just as Andrew said that, there was a knock on the door. Andrew shouted, "Come in!"

They both looked in the direction of the door. Then Andrew said, "Steven, my man! You got the stuff?"

"Yea, I got it," Steven replied.

"Cool." Andrew looked at Alexandria and said, "A l e x a n d r i a, will you be hanging tonight?"

"I guess," she replied hesitantly.

"You sure?" Steven asked Andrew.

"Yea, man," Andrew said getting up from the bed heading towards the door.

Alexandria didn't know what the plans were, and she didn't ask for details either.

As soon as they both left, she yelled out the door, "WHAT DO I NEED TO WEAR?"

"WHATEVER. WE'RE LEAVING AT 11!" Andrew yelled back.

**

Alexandria looked over at her nightstand and the time read 9:44PM. She had been talking to Landon for a couple of weeks, but they decided to take things slow for a while. It was working out better that way so far. Whenever they did talk, their conversations had more substance. Normally, Alexandria would wait for him to call or text, but she knew that he wouldn't be home for the break because he was working. She decided to just call him first, this time, to give him a piece of home.

Ring! Ring! Ring!

"Alex, Hey!"

"Hey!"

"Baby, you have no idea how good it is to hear your voice."

"Awe, well, I know you're not coming home for the holidays, and I know I'll get pretty busy here soon with the family. I wanted to call you and let you know that I was thinking about you."

"You know what?"

"What?"

"My mom and brother are actually coming down for Thanksgiving since I couldn't get off work! So, they should be here tomorrow evening."

"Oh, that's great! I'm hanging out with my brothers tonight. They actually have something planned. I don't know what it is though," she laughed.

"That's cool. I'm really glad that things are back good between you and Steven."

"Yea. Me too."

There was a silence on the phone. For some awkward reason, this conversation was different.

"Is everything ok?" Alexandria finally asked.

"Yea."

"OK. It just seems weird," she admitted.

"Lex, before you called, I was seriously sitting here wanting to call you. But I know that we decided that we would talk once a week and take things slow. I wanted to call you. I really miss you."

Alexandria didn't know what to say. They hadn't said that they loved each other again since they reconnected. When Landon first reached out to her a couple of weeks ago, he told her that he missed her, but they steered away from talks like that to keep their conversations more friendly.

Alexandria didn't know why she really called him, but she knew that she missed him. She refrained from saying anything; everything was perfectly fine the way it was.

"It just makes it hard fighting the fact that I still love you," Landon said breaking the silence.

Alexandria thought to herself, *What was he doing? I didn't want to ruin it.*

Then she quickly said, "Landon, I don't want to ruin a perfectly good thing."

"I get it."

Alexandria knew it was hard for Landon because it was hard for her too. They continued talking for a while until it was time for her to head out with Andrew and Steven.

The night felt especially dark, but for it being November, it wasn't too cold out.

"So, where are we going?" Alexandria asked as Steven was pulling out of the neighborhood.

"Alexandria, you gotta just ride," Andrew said.

As Steven drove the car, he blasted the music. It felt like the old days to Alexandria, except this time, she was in the back seat. She wasn't dressed up, so she only hoped that they weren't taking her to a club. But she was pretty sure that they wouldn't have let her leave the house looking so casual if we were going to be out with people.

She just sat there the entire ride until finally, Steven turned into a park. She had no idea what they were doing in the park so late, or why they were in the park at all. As Steven pulled into a parking spot, he turned the car off and went into his trunk. Andrew turned around and looked at her and said,

"Come on, let's take a walk."

Alexandria wasn't scared, but she was anxious to know what exactly they were getting ready to do.

"Where are we going, Drew?"

"Just follow me."

As she followed Andrew into the park, Steven followed close behind them. They walked through all the practice fields until they were in the middle of the park where the playground was. The grounds were still lit enough for them to see. Alexandria was so confused, but she knew that any question that she asked wouldn't get answered.

"Steven, hurry up man!" Andrew said as he looked back. Andrew then turned to Alexandria and asked, "Have you ever smoked before?"

She looked at him knowing that she was supposed to be a big girl now. "No... Y'all got weed?" She always wanted to try it, but no one ever let her do it.

"What you think?" Andrew responded.

Andrew took two brown rolled up things that looked like long tootsie rolls from Steven, and pulled a lighter out of his pocket.

"My man! You got that good stuff." Andrew said to Steven.

Alexandria looked at Steven and asked, "You smoke weed?"

"Oh no. I just supply the fun for the party. I prefer a wet pallet," he said, pulling out a flask from his back pocket.

Steven walked over to the merry-go-round and looked at Alexandria and said, "Alex, come get on."

She walked over, and Andrew followed as he lit up the tootsie roll like it was a cigarette. He sucked in, and the tip of it lit up. A few seconds later smoke came out his nose and mouth.

He extended it to Alexandria. "Here, hit it."

"Why does it look like that?" she asked.

"It's called a blunt," he said, handing her what now looked like a rolled up brown paper bag. She held it up, looking at it for a while. She had seen people smoke cigarettes before, so she just mimicked what she saw them do.

As she inhaled, Alexandria coughed out immediately after the first puff.

Andrew and Steven started laughing. Alexandria's chest felt like it was on fire, and she couldn't catch her breath.

"There you go," Andrew said as he took the blunt and hit it again. "You want to hit it again?" She looked at him. She finally stopped coughing and reached over for the blunt.

"I think she got it, bro," Andrew said to Steven.

"I think she's good for tomorrow," Steven said.

They all laughed aloud. The three of them stayed out in the park smoking and drinking until their eyes were red. They played on the swings and joked about the past, and it was the first time in a while that she forgot about everything going on.

CHAPTER 15

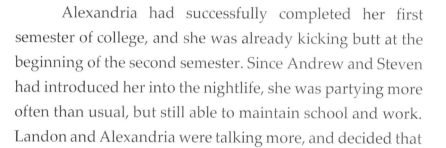

Alexandria had successfully completed her first semester of college, and she was already kicking butt at the beginning of the second semester. Since Andrew and Steven had introduced her into the nightlife, she was partying more often than usual, but still able to maintain school and work. Landon and Alexandria were talking more, and decided that since they managed the first semester of college successfully, it would be okay to take their relationship to the next level.

For some reason, the distance seemed to make their relationship work. They never fought, they were very understanding of each other's schedules, and they never went a day without speaking. It seemed like going to college somehow made their relationship more mature, and Alexandria really liked it. Although before Landon left, there were concerns about how he'd treated Alexandria while they were in high school, but there was something about his attentiveness to her now, that assured her that everything between them was really going to be fine.

Landon stayed off campus. He seemed to have going to work and school under control. Typically, he woke up early for school, and after classes, he went to work. They spoke in between those times; however, it was late at night when they were able to fill each other in about their entire day.

It was about an hour after they had ended their conversation that he called back.

"Everything ok?" Alexandria asked once she answered the phone.

"Yea - everything's fine."

"You're still up?" she asked with her tone dragging trying to make herself sound perky.

"Yea, I was about to go to sleep, but I just had to call you." His voice sounded really settled which threw her off because normally she could tell his emotions through the tone in his voice. "I miss you so much, Lex."

"Awe. Babe, I miss you too." Alexandria could feel his heart through the phone. She did miss Landon very much, and the fact that everything was going great made her miss him even more.

"We'll see each other soon," she said reassuring him.

"That's what I wanted to talk to you about...What do you think about coming down here for spring break?"

She was shocked because she hadn't given traveling to see Landon much thought.

Landon continued, "Why wait until the summer? I was looking, and we both go on break the same time."

Alexandria was still in disbelief. "Wow," she said quickly so he wouldn't think that she didn't like the idea. It had been months since she last saw Landon, and she was nervous.

"With the way things are now between us, it would be great. You could stay here with me in my apartment, and I can show you around."

"How will I get down there? I can't drive all the way down to Valdosta, Georgia alone."

"I know, but we can figure that out."

She began to get excited about the idea. She would finally see Landon again. They would finally be together again. "Let's do it!"

Alexandria managed to ease her mom into the idea of letting her go down there for the week, and she took the time off of work. Landon ended up coming up with the idea of taking the Greyhound bus service to travel down there. He purchased the ticket and sent her the information. Alexandria was a little nervous since she had never ridden the bus before, but she knew that it would be the only way to make this happen.

The day finally came for Alexandria to travel down to see him. Mrs. Anderson dropped her off at the station and as she hugged her mom goodbye, Mrs. Anderson said, "Alex, you be safe down there."

"I will."

"Call me when you get there."

"Ok."

When the bus was loading, Alexandria stepped onto the bus. She was so nervous to be leaving home. She kept telling herself, *this is that this was all part of growing up.*

ALEX:	Headed your way ☺
LANDON:	Waiting for you.
LANDON:	I love you.
ALEX:	I love you too.

The entire bus ride was uncomfortable, but she kept thinking in the back of her mind how there would only be a few more hours, and then Landon and she would be alone. It was a good thing that his roommate decided to go away on vacation during the break; especially since Landon had to work some hours so that he wouldn't fall behind on his rent.

Alexandria was so excited to see Landon. She knew that the next couple of days would set the tone for their future. She thought, *how cool would it be actually to marry my high school sweetheart?*

***

When the bus stopped, everyone started to gather their belongings. She was nervous to see Landon, ready to get off the bus and excited to see Landon all at the same time. As she stood in the line that was leading off the bus, she tried to look out the window, but the blinds were down to block the rays from the sun. As she got closer to the door, she thought to herself again, *calm down Lex, just be cool!* She wanted the week to be perfect.

As she stepped off the bus, she looked around, but didn't see Landon. She walked over to get her suitcase from under the bus and thought maybe she should call and see where he is. She decided not to call him earlier that day because she didn't want it to seem like she was bugging him. She trusted that he would be there. But then again, it's not like he had a car down there with him. As she was turning around to walk inside, Landon came out of nowhere with his arms wide opened.

"Landon! Oh my gosh!" she said aloud as he hugged her. It was so tight that her feet actually left the ground. She let go of her suitcase and tightly wrapped her arms around his neck.

When Landon finally let her go, he said, "You look amazing!"

"I'm so happy to see you, Babe. You have no idea!" Alexandria said smiling from ear to ear. She tightly held his waist from the side.

"You? I'm so happy you're here," he said looking down at her. She was gazing back at him, trusting that every step she was making was in the right direction.

"I got a taxi here, but it's not far from my apartment. He's parked right over there," he motioned with his head. As they got closer to the cab, Alexandria realized that all of her nervousness went away. She was so happy to be with Landon again. As he placed her suitcase in the trunk of the car, and he took her backpack off and walked towards the passenger side of the door. The trunk closed quickly and Landon walked towards her as he grabbed the door to open it. He took her backpack out of her hand and quickly leaned in, removing his other hand from the door and gently touching her chin to bring her head in for a kiss.

"I'm really glad you're here," he said. Alexandria smiled at him and knew that everything would be fine.

As they got into the taxi and drove off, Landon began to give her a mini tour, and before she knew it, they were stopping in a little town.

"So, you remember I told you that I stay in a loft?"

"Yea."

"Well, this is it. It's over this store. It's pretty big, you'll see."

Everything was entirely different than how she had imagined it. Once they were out of the taxi, Landon paid the driver, and then Alexandria followed him to the side of the building towards the stairs. It was pretty dark in the hallway, but he led the way. When they made it to the top, his front door was a few steps away.

Landon opened the door and walked in with her stuff as she followed. It was so weird to see him living on his own, but she could definitely tell that it helped him mature. After he had finished showing her around, he asked, "Are you hungry?"

Alexandria wasn't hungry. She just wanted to spend time with him.

"I'm not starving, but I can eat something," Alexandria responded.

"There's this spot that I want to take you to. It's in the town, and then after that, we can go see a movie or come back if you're tired."

"Let's do the movie. That sounds like fun."

"Cool."

It took Alexandria about an hour and a half to get ready after the long bus ride. By the time they actually left it was dinner time. As they walked outside, daylight was still out, and the weather wasn't too hot. The restaurant was four doors down. Once they were seated, Alexandria realized that she hadn't called her mom. She went to the restroom to make the call only to get Mrs. Anderson's voicemail.

When she got back to the table, Landon looked up and said, "You good?"

"Yep. I got her voicemail."

"So, what do you think so far?

"I like it. This is a pretty nice place. Do you eat here a lot?"

"Yea. It reminds me of a diner because of the menu, but it's nicer." They laughed as they looked over the menu.

After the waiter brought their orders, Landon said, "I have so much I want you to see while you're here," Landon told Alexandria as they sat eating.

"You're the main thing I want to see," Alexandria said.

***

The rest of the week exceeded her expectations. The day before she was supposed to leave, Landon had to work. She spent most of the day watching Netflix and the other part cleaning up and packing. It was dark out, and Alexandria was lying on the bed finishing up another movie when she heard the door open.

"Honey, I'm home!" Landon joked as he walked in. He made his way into the room and kissed her on the forehead.

"How was work?"

"It was good. How was your day? I see you cleaned. You didn't have to."

"I know, but I wanted to. I had a relaxing day, but I missed you...I'm not ready to leave," she whined.

"I know, I'm not ready for you to go either." He sat down on the bed as she sat up and paused the movie. "I've been thinking."

"What?" she said attentively, like a little child about to hear good news.

"Before you got here, I'll admit, I didn't know what would happen since it's been a minute since we saw each other."

Alexandria chuckled and said, "I was crazy nervous."

"But it's been better than before."

"It really has."

"I'm thinking about transferring back home after this semester."

"Really? Why?" Alexandria didn't want to totally think she was the reason. Actually, she hoped that she wasn't the reason - they were both doing so good, with the distance.

"Well for starters, it's expensive being down here. My mom can't really help me with rent and other bills, and I have to work a lot. I barely have time to study. At first, I thought we were coming here together, and then when everything happened, I came here to get away. But being here has made me realize that I really don't want to be away, especially from you."

Alexandria was touched to hear how much Landon wanted to be back home.

"So, you're gonna move back home?"

"Well, for now that's the plan. Me and a couple of boys here just want to be in the city, and having three roommates would be cheaper than just one. Plus, the city would be more expensive."

"Where would you go to school, state?"

"I wanna go to school with you."

"Babe, I think it's a great idea. I just want you to know what you're doing."

"Me and the guys talked about it, but how do you feel about it?"

"I miss you a lot. Honestly, everything for me back home is good. It would be different having you home with the fact that we've done the long distance thing for nearly a year. But I would be kidding myself if I said I didn't want you closer!"

Something in Alexandria just wouldn't settle. She felt uneasy about the situation. Landon grabbed her hand and said, "Listen babe, eventually, I would want for us to get a place together," Alexandria was shocked.

"That's a pretty big step," she said looking directly into his eyes.

"I mean, I know. It's not tomorrow, but I know that I want to marry you. There's no other girl for me."

Alexandria couldn't help but smile.

"Wow, I think it's great," she replied.

"We'll be okay." It was like Landon could sense she wasn't totally sold on the city life. "Lex, you will be my wife."

"Don't say things you can't promise, Landon."

"Alexandria, you are my wife."

He leaned in again to kiss her, and cradle her as they fell back onto the bed. They made love that night. It wasn't their first time, but it was the first time she knew it was more than just experimenting or being horny. They really loved each other, and it was the deepest way they know how to express that love.

CHAPTER 16

Alexandria finally finished her first year of college. It was a successful year. She was anticipating Landon's arrival in a few days. Ever since she came back home from spring break, things between them remained really good. She continued to hang out with a few people from school, and they all decided to meet after finals to celebrate the end to a great year. There was a guy named Robbie that was in Alexandria's study group that she tends to speak to the most about her relationship with Landon.

That afternoon at lunch, they were sitting in the group, and everyone was having different side conversations as they waited for their food.

Alexandria was asked, "So, Alexandria, are you ready for Landon to come home?"

"Yea, of course," she answered. Robbie gave her a look out of the corner of his eye.

"Listen. I don't want to kill your vibe, but I'm from a small town. It's boring there."

Alexandria turned to converse with him directly.

"Robbie, I already know how you feel about Landon. But like I told you before, you don't even know him."

"Landon loves you. But you're so level headed and mature. He's still growing up."

Alexandria laughed at him. "You're still growing, Robbie."

"I know. That's why I'm saying it."

"We will be ok," she patted him on the shoulder as she turned to face everyone else at the table.

Normally, Alexandria would get annoyed when people tried to doubt her relationship choice, but she knew that Robbie was only speaking from his heart. He didn't know the history Landon and she had. She was anxious to start this next chapter of their relationship. Growing up in their relationship wasn't the easiest, but she was determined to see it out as long as she could.

***

Landon made it into town, but with all the moving, they decided to meet up later on in the week. The summer was amazing, it was better than ever, and Alexandria couldn't wait to start school and introduce Landon to everyone. After that first year, so many students transferred out and in; however, it was Alexandria's last year at the school, and she was very excited about knocking it out of the park.

Most of Landon's credits had transferred, so he wasn't too far behind. They didn't have any classes together, but their schedules were in sync so that they could be in school during the same time. She had grown accustomed to her school, but she could only imagine that it was different from the school he'd transferred from.

Alexandria was sitting in the cafeteria waiting on Landon, a random guy came and sat down at the table;

"Hey. I think we have a class together."

"Oh really, which one?" She typically asked because that threw guys off who are just trying to hit on her.

"You're in Professors Chen's chemistry class?"

Alexandria chuckled because they did actually have a class together. "Yea, I'm in his class."

"I'm Trent. What's your name?" he introduced himself.

"Alexandria."

"Cool. Well, you always seem so focused in class, so I know you are getting all the information. Maybe we can form a study group because I gotta pass this course."

"Yea, that sounds cool."

Just as they were finishing their conversation, a girl walked up and gave him a hug and a kiss on the cheek.

"Hey Honey!"

"Hey, Babe, this is Alexandria from my chemistry class."

"Hey, Alexandria! I'm Courtney," she said all full of life and kissed him again and said, "I gotta go. I will call you later. Nice to meet you, Alexandria."

"You too," Alexandria responded.

As she took off as quickly as she came, Trent said, "She took off like a lightning bolt, huh?" They both started laughing.

"Yea."

"That's my girl."

"Oh okay, cool. I am actually waiting for my boyfriend to get out of class, which should have been already."

"Oh, well, I'll catch up with you in class."

Just as Trent was walking away, Alexandria saw Landon walking up. He seemed a little upset.

"Hey, babe. You alright?" she asked.

"Yea, I'm good. Who was that?"

"I just met him from my chemistry class." She could tell Landon was annoyed. "Are you sure you're okay?"

"Alex, if I say I'm ok, trust that I'm ok."

"Okay. Sorry." She sat there as Landon sat across the table. He placed both elbows on the table and held his head. Alexandria didn't want to pry, but she could tell something was bothering him. She just knew he didn't want to talk about it, and it bothered her, but she didn't want to argue about something that could possibly be nothing at all.

Since Landon had been back, they had spent a lot of idle time together. They couldn't really go out on dates because he didn't like for her to pay all the time, and he was having a hard time finding a job. She knew he was becoming frustrated because things weren't moving as smoothly as he'd hoped. She just tried to make the time that they spent together relaxed.

***

A few weeks went by, and things started to get pretty tense with Landon's situation. They were sitting in the cafeteria at school, and Alexandria worked on school work with the time that she had in between classes. Landon and she had been talking and not talking all at the same time. It seemed that they were dancing around an issue that was building. And the bad part about it is she had no idea what it was. She remained quiet most of the time.

"Are you happy?" he looked up from his book and asked her. She was surprised because she didn't think she was giving him the impression that she wasn't happy.

"Of course. I'm just focused because I'm studying, but I'm happy."

"I mean with life, Lex?"

"Yea, I'm happy. What's there not to be happy about? I'm alive. I'm in a great relationship, and the list goes on."

Alexandria wanted to ask him if he was happy. She knew he had something to say, but she was really afraid of the answer.

"I'm thinking I'm going to drop my classes this semester," Landon said.

"Why? What happened?"

"A few weeks ago, they dropped my classes due to non-payment. I had to add the classes to my schedule again because they messed up my financial aid. I've spent so much time trying to fix it, I fell behind. The withdrawal period is coming up, and I just feel like it's the best decision.

"Did you try talking to your professors?"

"What do you think I'm dumb, Alex! Of course, I tried talking to them." Alexandria was confused, and Landon was getting louder, and she didn't want to get in a fight or make a scene in the cafeteria.

"Will you come back next semester?"

"I mean, yea. I also picked classes with your schedule, and I don't have the same work hours as you. Most of the jobs I can get right now don't work with my current school schedule." Alexandria sat there, listening. "I need to work because my mom keep talking about me moving back home and how I need to be working, and on top of that, I can't take you out like I want." Landon looked to her to say something, but she didn't know what to say, and she didn't want to say the wrong thing.

"What do you think?" he asked after waiting a while for her response.

Alexandria didn't want to tell him what she thought. She thought he should stay in school and finish the semester and then set his schedule to work next semester. She wanted him to be ok with her covering some of their dates because they were in this together. She wanted him to know that whatever was bothering him at home would be over soon enough. But instead, she said, "It's ultimately up to you."

He chuckled. "Really, that's your answer? It's up to

me. Why the hell you press me to talk to you, and then when I do, you give me bullshit answers like that? I know who it's up to, I asked you what you thought." He was stern in his tone and people around them could now hear the conversation.

"Calm down."

"Alex, don't tell me to calm down." Landon said sounding even more frustrated than before.

"I think we should probably have this conversation somewhere else," Alexandria said as she began to close her books.

"Why?"

"Because you're being loud and it's embarrassing."

"Oh, I'm embarrassing you?"

"Oh my gosh! Landon. Really?" she said as she unzipped her backpack and placed it on the table.

"Yea. Maybe if you get embarrassed you will stop entertaining these other guys in here like you don't already have a man."

Alexandria stopped packing her things for a moment and looked at Landon.

"Seriously? What are you talking about??"

Alexandria became annoyed that he found pleasure in taking his anger out on her. She stood up from the table to put her things away to leave, but before she knew it, Landon had stood up. He flipped the table over, and all of her books fell to the floor, along with her calculator, which broke. Alexandria quickly bent down to pick up her things, trying not to make eye contact with the room full of students that had now grown quiet. Out of the corner of her eye, she saw Landon quickly take off out the door.

"What a jerk! Are you ok?"

"Yea, I'm fine," she responded still looking down to get her things in her bag. She picked the table up and placed it back where it was.

"Here you go." Alexandria finally looked up, and saw that it was Courtney. She was handing Alexandria batteries that came out of her now broken calcuator.

"Thanks. Courtney, right?

"Yea."

"I've got to go," Alexandria said and quickly left the cafeteria. On her way to her car, she was startled by a beckoning voice from behind her.

"Ma'am!"

The voice seemed to be getting closer, so she stopped

and turned around. It was the campus police officer.

"Ma'am, are you alright?"

"Yes, sir. I'm fine." Alexandria was nervous because she knew they had caused a scene, but she didn't want them to get in any trouble.

"Do you know the person that just did that?"

"Barely," Alexandria lied.

"Are you sure you are ok? Because we can definitely conduct an investigation," the officer assured her.

"Honestly, I'm fine. There's no need for that. It won't happen again."

"Ok. Well, you can come see me if you ever feel like you're in danger or this person is a danger to the campus."

"Yes, sir."

"You have a good afternoon."

"Thanks. You too."

Alexandria could feel her heart beating like it was about to burst out of her chest. She quickly headed for her car. She knew it would be best if she laid low for the remainder of the day. She and Landon normally drove to school together since their classes were around the same time, but when she got to the car, he wasn't there. She had two more classes that day, but sh didn't feel up to going. She just wanted to get out of there, so she texted Landon.

ALEX: Where are you?

ALEX: I'm ready to go home.

Landon didn't respond, so she got in her car and waited. About an hour later, there was a knock on the passenger side window. It was Landon. Alexandria unlocked the door to let him in.

"Landon, have you completely lost your mind?"

He didn't say anything to her. She turned the car on, and they drove home in silence. When they finally made it to his house, Landon looked over to her and said, "I'm sorry. I just got a lot of stuff going on right now."

"I know." Deep down, Alexandria could sense Landon wanted to be back out on his own, and the fact that he couldn't do that was adding to the frustration. She just didn't understand why he would take it out on her. She decided that she would choose her words wisely until this passed.

***

Landon withdrew from school. He was able to get a warehouse job that was paying him good money, but it meant they saw each other less. Alexandria ended up missing most of her classes, telling herself that she would study and go back for the scheduled quizzes and tests. When she wasn't at school, she spent her time with Landon. She became completely distracted with trying to help him.

One morning, she stopped by Landon's house, on the way to school after he'd gotten off work. She crawled into the bed with him to cuddle for a while.

He held Alexandria in his arms for a moment and then whispered in her ear, "I know things have been a little tough. But I want to take you out this weekend."

She quickly turned over to look at him.

"Really?"

"Yea, I got something planned."

"I'd really love that," she said as she hugged him and gave him a kiss. Alexandria couldn't wait for the weekend. They hadn't talked about the incident that happened in the cafeteria, but Landon seemed much happier working.

Landon picked her up, and they went out to an arcade and bowling alley. They were having a great time playing the arcade games. Hunger struck, so they headed to the bar to get something to eat.

"Alex!?"

It was Jay from the party years back.

"Oh my gosh, Jay? What's up?"

"It's been a while, girl. How you been?"

"I've been good. This is my boyfriend, Landon."

"What's up, man. I'm, Jay. I met Alex through a mutual friend."

"Cool," Landon said.

"I didn't know you worked here."

"Yea, I pick up extra hours here in the bar on the weekends. But, um, let me know when you're are ready to order. I got you."

Alexandria looked at Landon, who was sitting there listening. Once Jay left, he started talking.

"So, who's the mutual friend?"

"Kim." Alexandria replied nonchalantly.

"Oh, that's one of her little boyfriends?"

She didn't want to tell Landon exactly how she knew Jay, but she didn't want anything to come back up later either.

"No, he's a friend of one of her little boyfriends," She laughed, trying to blow it over. Landon didn't press the issue which was great. After they'd placed their orders,

Landon, who normally didn't drink much had a few more drinks than normal.

"Babe. I think you should slow down."

"Chill."

"Ok, then let me drive."

They were both buzzed, but Alexandria could handle her liquor better than him.

"I'm good." Then Landon motioned to Jay. "Aye, man, ain't she sexy?"

"OK, Landon. Let's go."

"Let him answer," Landon said.

"I think you should listen to your girl, man," Jay responded.

As Alexandria began to pull Landon so they could leave, he turned around and laughed at her. "Isn't it funny how you always got people coming up to you?"

"No one is coming up to me, Landon."

As they were walking through the arcade, Landon spotted a group of girls and walked over to them. Landon was buzzed, but Alexandria knew he wasn't drunk.

"Which one of you sexy ladies want to come home with me tonight?"

"Really?" Alexandria said as she walked away towards the car and left him standing there.

She stood at the car for about 10 minutes before Landon came out.

"Oh, you still here?" he asked her.

"Well, that's a crazy question. How am I supposed to leave? We drove here together on a date, genius."

"Oh, you're the genius. You got *everything* together."

Landon opened the driver side, got in and turned the car on.

"Landon, stop playing and open the door," she yelled. Landon put the car in reverse and began to back out of the parking space. "Landon! Stop it!"

Landon rolled down his passenger window and said, "You can figure this out, genius."

"What the hell is your problem?" Alexandria asked with frustration.

Landon then put the car in drive and drove off. She stood there hoping that he would turn around, but 30 minutes went by, and he didn't come back. Alexandria was trying to be understanding of the changes that Landon was going through since the move but she was so over this stupid roller coaster.

How could he be so buzzed that he'd drive off and leave me in the middle of the parking lot?

She needed to clear her head; she didn't sign a contract to be a part of this movie that Landon was getting in. Alexandria thought, *this only happens in movies!*

She got out her phone and called the only person that she knew would come get her and take her mind off things.

CHAPTER 17

———～———

Alexandria had spent the night tossing and turning. She couldn't really get a good nights rest.

"Are you okay?" Kimberly asked as she was woken to Alexandria getting up from the bed and going to the bathroom for what seemed the 100th time.

"I'm getting there."

Alexandria felt so stupid, being left out there all alone. She knew Kimberly didn't judge her, but she had hoped that Landon knew by now that every time someone had to save her from something he did, it made him look bad.

"Listen, Lex. What we need to do is hit up a few clubs tonight. Get your mind off this Landon drama. Are you down with that?"

"Yea," she responded faintly as she picked up her phone to see if Landon had at least text. Alexandria was angry with him, but there wasn't much she could do. She called, but got no response in return. Since Landon wanted to do whatever he wanted, then she was determined that she was going to do the same.

**

Kimberly and Alexandria were shopping at the mall. While shopping, they ran into Steven and his girlfriend. Over the Thanksgiving break, Alexandria was able to get to know Steven's girlfriend much better. They invited Kimberly and Alexandria to meet up before heading to the club.

"Lex, I hope you ready!" Kimberly said. She was always the one Alexandria turned to when she wanted to forget about her problems, because Kimberly made sure she lived in the moment.

They worked up an appetite looking for their outfits for the club that night so they left to grab lunch.

As they ate, they talked about the night before.

"I just can't believe he left you in the parking lot! I mean, how did he expect you to get home?"

"Kim, your guess is as good as mine. I think the worst part is that he hasn't even called to check up on me."

"Lex, what are you going to do? This guy is a freakin' psycho."

Alexandria hated that people were actually starting to dislike her and Landon's relationship. She wanted everyone to still believe they were the hottest couple.

"What else can I do, Kim? I'm just going to try and move on with my life. Clearly, Landon's going through something right now."

"Well, Alex darling, he's not going to take up another second of my day. Tonight, we gonna let loose and gonna get turnt."

***

They were getting ready for the club, and Landon was blowing Alexandria's phone up.

"Ugh! Lex, don't answer his call. What he got, ESP? He just know you bout to go out, hug?"

Alexandria wanted to answer the phone, but she knew that it would be best if she just waited until the morning. Landon kept calling until finally he got the hint that I didn't want to talk, then he called Kimberly.

Annoyed Kimberly answered, "What do you want?"

"Hey, Kim! How are -"

"Good, Landon. I'm doing just fine," she interrupted him. "What do you want?"

She'd put the phone on speaker phone on so that her friend could hear the conversation.

"Have you heard from Alex?"

"Oh, you mean since you left her in the parking lot and didn't check up on her and had me have to get out of my warm bed to pick her up because you decided to be crazy? Yea, she's with me, asshole!"

"I'm sorry about all that, Kim. But I really need to talk to her and she's not answering. I really need to talk to her; she's not answering."

"Oh, that's great. Why should she answer, Landon? Give me one good reason she should answer, and I'll make sure she calls you."

"Because, Kim. Stop playin'."

"That's funny. You think I'm playin'?" Kimberly shot back.

"I should've known she was with your evil self."

"Wrong answer."

Kimberly hung the phone up on Landon and he called back, but she refused to answer. He kept calling.

"Girl, get rid of this roach! He is NOT gonna to keep calling my phone all night."

Alexandria answered Kimberly's phone.

"Hello?" She didn't know which field to play. Angry girlfriend or understanding because she wanted to talk.

"Kim, I was just playing around." Landon pleaded.

"This is Alex," she said softly.

"Alex, Babe, you're not answering my phone calls. You know I'm sorry about last night."

"Landon, you have to stop calling Kim's phone. I'll call you back tomorrow. We can talk then."

"Why we can't talk now?"

"Because. I'm with Kim right now."

"Well, I'm coming over then."

"No. You're not. We won't even be here. We're about to leave."

"Where are you going?"

"Out, Landon."

"You know I don't like you hanging out with Kim. Y'all gonna be with that dude from the bar?"

"No. Landon, I have to go."

"I'm coming over."

"I'm telling you now; we won't be here."

"Well, wait for me then."

Kimberly grabbed the phone. "This is my phone. Goodbye, Landon. And don't bother calling her phone either, because I will have it tonight." She hung up.

Moments later they left Kimberly's house and headed for Steven's girlfriend's apartment. Once they arrived, the apartment was already full of people, and everyone was drinking and smoking.

"Come on, Lex. Let's get it in now before we get to the club."

Kimberly headed straight for the liquor table and Alexandria followed behind her. They had been clubbing all year together, but they never got this lit before going. Before they got to the apartment, Alexandria called a couple of friends to meet them there. Everyone left the apartment, piling into cars with designated drivers heading to the club.

The night was one for the books. They took over every VIP section and there were so many promotors trying to connect with them. Alexandria danced the night away. Anytime they went out, Alexandria always felt weird dancing with other guys, so she danced with Steven or one of the her friends.

They stayed out until the club was about to close, and then they went back to the apartment to crash for the night. Alexandria was so tired that she didn't even think to check her phone to see if Landon called.

***

Alexandria got up late. The next morning we woke up late, and I finally looked at her phone. She'd missed several calls from Landon. Alexandria figured she would just give him a call once she made it back home; that way he would be able to come over if he still wanted to talk.

On the way home, after they woke up, Kimberly and Alexandria had another talk.

"Lex. I don't think we ever partied that hard before. Your brother is a party animal, man."

"I know! right? I had fun though," Alexandria said smiling.

"That's good."

"I woke up this morning to a ton of phone calls and messages from Landon."

"Did you call him back, yet?"

"Nope. I figured I would just give him a call once I got home."

"Lex, I want you to know that I love you and Landon; but when are you going to stop allowing him to act this way? These tantrums are too much, and I know that he wasn't always like this."

"I know. I'm trying to see if he just needs the time to adjust to the changes, but it's like he takes all his frustration out on me. And let's not forget his jealousy issues."

"Don't you think he's a bit controlling?"

"He is very protective, and I haven't given him a reason to think that I need protection. Everyone that I talk to knows that I have a boyfriend."

"Girl, he treats you as if you act the way he does! I'm gonna to tell you like this, don't allow him to make you think that you're the reason he's acting like that. He's a grown man; he knows how to act."

"I know."

"You're so loyal though, so I know you want to fight it out. But just be smart. It's a dangerous line you cross when he feels like it's okay to treat you this way. And he only thinks it's okay because you let him get away with it."

"You're right."

As they were finishing their conversation, they pulled up into Kimberly's driveway, and Landon's car was parked outside.

"What the hell is he doing here?" Kimberly asked.

"I guess I should have called him back."

"Girl, I am going inside. I cannot deal with him right now. Let me know if you need anything."

"Ok."

Kimberly put her car in park, and they both started getting out of the car. Landon started to get out of his as well. Kimberly went into her house through the garage, while I walked towards Landon.

"Wow, Alex, if I knew you were partying like that while I was away, I would have reconsidered coming back."

"Hey, Landon." Alexandria said ignoring his statement.

"You're ignoring me. You know I hate that."

She was a little frustrated because he was trying to glaze over the fact that he'd left her in the parking lot.

"Landon, you left me in a parking lot without a simple courtesy call to check in and see if I at least made it home safely."

"Alex, give it a rest. You know I was drunk. I barely remember the other night."

"And that makes it ok?" Alexandria said annoyed.

"No. I'm sorry about that."

"You're always sorry."

"I stayed here last night waiting on you," Landon told her.

"I didn't ask you to do that. As a matter of fact, I told ou not to come.""

"So, what, we're not together anymore? You let me know." Alexandria just stared at him. She didn't say anything. "You don't have anything to say?"

She remained silent. Then after a few minutes said, "I don't want to fight with you, Landon. Let's just talk about this a little later."

"No, let's talk about it now."

Alexandria didn't have much to say to Landon. At that moment, she felt numb to everything he was saying. She reached into her purse to pull out a cigarette.

"Since when you smoke?" Landon pried.

She didn't answer him, but stood there with the cigarette in her hand. Landon had picked up smoking cigarettes before leaving to go to college. She just never entertained the habit until she started going out more.

Alexandria began to look around wondering to herself *what she was doing with my life*. She hadn't been to class and was falling behind. She was partying, drinking and smoking more than she did in her entire life. She wanted to be with Landon, but it seemed as though he only wanted to be with her when it was convenient for him.

"Why are you ignoring me?" Landon quizzed.

Alexandria could see that Landon was getting angry, but she didn't have anything to say to him. She thought to herself, *did he want me to say that I started smoking because his mood swings stressed me out?*

"I don't know why I'm smoking, Landon. It just calms my nerves," Alexandria said calmly.

"Why you nervous?" he said, looking at her sternly with his back pressed up against his car. She didn't want to answer the question because every answer would point to him. She didn't want to say any of it verbally. It was better left unsaid. For some reason, she still wanted to be with him; she just didn't like the person he was.

"Don't you hear me talking to you?!" He balled his fits as though he wanted to punch something.

Alexandria wanted to be honest with him, but she knew that at that moment it wouldn't help. She felt so out of control, like she was in a car that was getting ready to crash into a brick wall, and she was refusing to put her foot on the brakes.

Tears began to swell up in her eyes as she held in all the emotions. She didn't know what was wrong with Landon. She didn't know why he was mad all the time. Realistically, you could say that they were growing apart; however, she knew that wasn't it. She felt like there was a life he wanted that was battling the life he had, but she didn't understand why she was in the middle. Alexandria loved him through some tough times. She had been there for a while. Alexandria loved him, and she fought to hold the tears back as Landon walked closer to her.

He grabbed her face really hard and out of nowhere BIT HER CHEEK! All the tears that she was holding started to roll out of her eyes.

"Landon!" she screamed as she pushed him away. "Why would you do that? That hurt!"

"You don't care, right? Nothing bothers you?"

"So, you bite me!?" Alexandria yelled. "I never told you I didn't care or that things don't bother me!" she said crying. She was so confused as she held her cheek and turned to walk away from Landon. Then he came behind her and held her really tight in his arms.

"I'm sorry," he said.

Alexandria didn't want to ask, what for? So, she just cried in silence. Without fighting his grip, they stood in that position for a while until Landon asked, "Do you want to come home with me so we can really talk about us?"

"I'll get Kim to take me home, and then I will come over later on so I can change and get my car."

"Ok. I will see you later," he whispered in her ear as kissed her cheek and loosed her from his grip. She slowly turned around as she heard him quickly get into his car. She watched as he pulled off and then she went through the garage into the house.

Alexandria closed the door and headed straight to the bathroom to wash her face before heading upstairs. When she got upstairs, Kim was sitting on the bed on the phone.

"Kevin, I will hit you up a little later, my girl just walked in." Kimberly hung up and asked, "Is everything ok?"

"Yea, Landon just left."

"What did he say?"

"That he's sorry."

"Shocker."

Alexandria knew that Kimberly's sarcastic remark was right. She just couldn't get her heart and head to line up.

"Girl, let's light one up, then go get something to eat and then, if you want, you can come with me over to Kevin's house."

"Actually, Imma freshen up and grab that bite with you, but I really need some time to think."

"That's cool. I get it."

Kimberly and Alexandria got dressed and went out to her patio to smoke before heading out. They were pretty blazed, but they decided to go somewhere near my house to grab something to eat.

"So, what's good here?" Kimberly asked.

"I've tried pretty much everything on the menu. It's all pretty good," Alexandria replied.

"Ok, cool," Kimberly said as she skimmed through the menu. "So, are you going to see him today?"

"I think so. We still have some things to talk about. I think if we can talk through most of this, we would be ok."

"But I thought you told me in the car that you didn't feel like talking."

"Yea, I don't feel like talking about my feelings to him. But he needs to tell me what's bothering him."

"Gotcha."

A few minutes later, our waiter came to our table for their orders. She looked at me and said, "You're Alexandria, right?"

"Yea." Alexandria replied, "Your face looks so familiar."

"We went to high school together; I was an underclassman, but I saw you around. You dated Landon, right?"

"Yea. I'm sorry, what's your name again?"

"Gorgie."

"Right. I remember seeing you around. Good seeing you!"

"You too! I'll put your order in, and come back with your drinks."

As she turned to walk away, Kimberly leaned in and asked, "How awkward was that?"

"Very. I actually know of her because she hung with the girl that Landon got pregnant. She's also known for being a hoe."

"Are you serious?" Kimberly asked shocked.

"Yes!" Alexandria replied.

They both started laughing hysterically. Alexandria went to the restroom to wash her hands before the food got to the table. She was washing her hands when Gorgie walked in.

"Hey, again!" Alexandria joked.

"Hey - I wanted to ask you a question, and when I saw you come into the restroom, I figured I'd ask you here instead of in front of your friend."

"Oh, what's up?"

"Are you still with, Landon? I know he went away to college, and then he moved back home."

"Why?" Alexandria asked annoyed.

"Well, I heard he was back with you, but I wasn't sure. But, two nights ago he called me and asked me to come over."

"Interesting. Did you go?"

"Listen, I'm not trying to start anything. But I'm not the only one he's contacted. I talked to Landon for a couple of weeks, but if he's with you, which I think he is, you should know."

"Well, isn't that sweet of you," Alexandria said, drying her hands as she pretended she wasn't bothered by Gorgie's confession.

As Alexandria walked toward the door and pulled it open, Gorgie said from behind her, "But to answer your question, No. I didn't go over."

Alexandria walked back to the table with her nerves bad and heart racing. She told Kimberly she needed to step outside for a second. Alexandria needed a cigarette. She didn't know if she should confront Landon about it then or wait until later. She knew he would deny it, but how would she know that none of the other girls didn't actually go over and meet with him.

Alexandria didn't tell Kimberly about the conversation she I had with Gorgie in the restroom. After lunch, Kimberly dropped Alexandria off at home. She quickly gathered some clothes to stay over at Landon's that night and head to work the next morning. As she pulled up to Landon's house, she reminded herself to play it cool. She wanted to know how their relationship would play out, but she didn't want to be the nagging girlfriend.

Landon and Alexandria talked that afternoon about his leaving her in the parking lot. She even brought up Gorgie, and he denied that it ever happened. To her, it seemed as though their relationship was starting to be about making up. She asked Landon if he was bored in bed.

"Girl, don't ask me anything crazy like that."

But Alexandria really wanted to know. She felt like Landon loved her but still wanted to explore. However, that was just something she couldn't find myself asking him. That night she said a little prayer. Alexandria promised God that if He'd fix her relationship, then she wouldn't have sex anymore. She knew that the decision to lose her virginity to Landon, when they weren't married, wasn't Christian behavior at all.

Alexandria knew it was a selfish thing to pray considering that she wasn't the only one in the relationship, but she knew that if God fixed their relationship, wanting to wait to have sex should be understandable. She didn't know what else to do. She and Landon wanted to be in the same room, but they were far from ok. It was like they'd learned to live in their dysfunction.

Night had come, and Landon sat on the edge of the bed listening to music on his laptop. Alexandria laid in the bed with her head at the foot of it, with her back turned to Landon. There was a cold breeze on her. Landon pulled the covers up and wrapped his arms around her waist, then started to slip his hand up her shirt. She gently moved his hand as she said, "Not tonight, Landon."

All Alexandria could think about was, *what if he'd been with other girls. What if I'm not pleasing him sexually.* I've laid there before not wanting to have sex because he wanted to.

Tonight she'd made up her mind that she wouldn't have sex. She just wanted to lie there and know that it was enough, that she was enough. Alexandria wanted to hear him talk about his issues, but he didn't want to talk. So, she laid there.

Landon quickly got up. "What you mean, not tonight?"

"I just don't want to have sex tonight."

Landon became furious. "Get the hell up then!"

"Landon, calm down. It's 1:30 in the morning."

"Get your shit, and get out!"

"Are you serious right now?"

"You probably messing with someone else anyways. Always hanging with that hoe, Kim – GET UP!"

Landon went into the closet and got Alexandria's things and threw her bags on the bedroom floor. "Alex, get out before I call the cops."

It was 1:30 in the morning. She couldn't go home now because it was too late, and he knew that. She slowly got out of the bed and walked into the closet.

"Where are you going?" he asked her.

"Landon, I have some things in here!" Alexandria didn't have anything in the closet; he'd thrown everything on the floor, but she wanted to divert the situation from the bedroom so Landon would at least have a moment to think about the fact that he was kicking her out of his house.

"Ain't nothing in there!" He left the bedroom and grabbed his cell phone. Seconds later she heard him say, "Yes, there is someone in my house that won't leave!" As he walked back into the room, he said, "Alex, I'm not going to ask you again to leave."

"Where exactly should I go?"

"I don't care! You just can't stay here." He hung up the phone.

"Did you just call the cops on me?"

"Yea, I called the cops. Get the hell out!"

"Alright, since you're serious. I want everything back. I WANT EVERYTHING BACK!!!" Alexandria wanted everything she ever gave him, every shoe, every shirt, EVERYTHING!!! She walked back into the closet to reclaim the things she had bought. If he wanted to end their relationship by calling the cops, Alexandria felt that was fine, but she wasn't about to walk out empty handed. He followed behind and grabbed her from behind and pushed her into the closet wall. He then grabbed her head and hit it on the wall. The hit was so hard she felt it in her nose.

Alexandria pushed Landon away from her only

wishing that his mom was there that night. As his hand grabbed her throat, she remained silent, as though she didn't want to scream to wake the neighbors.

"Get the hell out of my house!" Alexandria tried to move his hand, but she got light headed and began to blackout. Her legs began to buckle, and she fell to the ground. It was then that he released his grip and she gasped for air. Tears rolled down her cheeks.

Alexandria crawled out of the closet, and saw Landon grabbing her things from the middle of the floor. She quickly grabbed her cell phone and dialed 9-1-1.

"9-1-1, what's your emergency?"

"I need help. I'm having trouble breathing. The guy I'm with just pushed me into the wall."

Even at that moment, Alexandria was still trying to protect Landon. She wanted to scare him into stopping, but she didn't know what he would do.

"Ma'am, are you ok?"

"Yes."

"Are any children involved?"

"No."

As the operator was talking, Alexandria got up to

follow Landon to see what he was doing. He was taking all of her things out of the bag and throwing them out of his front door.

"He's destroying my stuff!"

"Ma'am, where exactly are you?"

"I don't know. Ridgewater."

"Ma'am, do you know the house number."

"No," Alexandria lied. She knew exactly where she was. She just wanted Landon to stop. Tears were coming down faster than ever, and she could barely catch her breath. She walked past Landon to hurry up and leave before the cops actually showed up.

"So, you gonna call the cops on me?" he yelled.

Alexandria walked to her car in the driveway. She decided just to leave everything.

"So you gonna call the cops on me?!" he yelled again. He ran up to her and grabbed her arms. She could see the anger in his eyes.

"Landon, just let me leave before they get here." Alexandria pleaded.

"Nah! Since you wanna call the cops, let me do something worth you calling 'em."

Landon threw Alexandria into the garage door, and she fell into the plants on the side of the house. She knew the cops would come any moment; she knew she shouldn't fight back. Alexandria didn't want to fight, she just wanted things to be good between them again. Landon balled his fist, and she immediately covered my face. He struck her on her leg first, and she instantly felt the throbbing of pain. She moved her hands to guard her legs, but then he struck her again on her arm. It hurt her so bad, but all Alexandria could do was roll over and quickly get up only to have Landon grab her by her head and throw her up against the side of the house.

Landon placed his hands on both sides of her so she couldn't move, and she could barely stand. He looked at her and said;

"Look what you done."

"Landon, please just leave before they come." Alexandria cried. He was biting his lower lip as she swiped the tears from her face. At that moment, they saw the blue lights and a bright light shine on her face from the car. Landon backed away as a cop approached us; he had a taser pointed in Landon's direction.

"Sir. Do you have a weapon?"

"No," Landon said.

***

The officer spoke to us individually. He asked Alexandria if she wanted to press charges, and she told him, no.

Then the officer looked at me and said, "Well, I didn't see him put his hands on you, but I did see the fear in your eyes when I arrived. According to the law, we have the right to press charges against him from the state, so he will be going in tonight."

Alexandria couldn't believe what she was hearing. She pleaded with the officer. She knew that this would ruin their relationship. She didn't want Landon to go! She watched as the officer handcuffed him and placed him in the backseat of the police car. As they drove off, she picked up the phone and called the only person she knew that could help, Kimberly.

Within the next couple of minutes, Alexandria met Kimberly at Liz's house. Kim called Steven on her way to meet Alexandria, who immediately called Andrew.

"Alex, when he gets out of jail, we're going after him."

Alexandria couldn't even argue. Her brothers were furious, and at that point, everything was falling apart.

"This isn't the first time this shit has happened, Lex! Why are you still with this clown?" Kimberly interjected while pacing back and forth.

Alexandria didn't have an answer. She just sat there on the front porch stairs as they planned their next move.

Steven finally looked at her and said, "Lex, baby girl, what do you want?"

She looked at Steven as he looked her in the eyes.

He continued, "If you want us to go after him, we will. But if we go after him and you get back with him, I'm going to be very angry with you."

She sat there, listening to them talk.

"Well?" Steven quizzed.

Even though Alexandria knew they didn't want to hear this answer, she didn't want her brothers to do anything that could get them in trouble or mess up her relationship with Landon, that was now hanging on by a thread.

"Just leave him alone." Alexandria whispered.

CHAPTER 18

That night, Alexandria couldn't get any sleep. She reached out to Landon's friends and his mom; everyone was furious with her. She stayed with Kimberly, and the next morning Kimberly drove her to the detention center to see about getting information.

Finally, Alexandria got some answers. They were able to tell her that Landon was still in custody and hadn't made bail. She knew his family was going through some financial issues at the time, and so she wasn't sure if they were going to be able to get him out. Since no one was taking my calls, she decided to go to the bail bondsmen myself.

Alexandria gave them all the information, and it was only a couple of thousands of dollars. She had been working and not spending much, so she had the money to post bail to get him out. That was the least she could do since she got him into the mess.

"Lexi, are you sure you want to do this?"

"I feel like I have to. No one else wants to help him."

"You don't know that."

Alexandria didn't know what to do. She thought, "If I got him out, would that constitute that we would still be together? Were we even together?" She had no idea. All she knew was that she loved him. She didn't care what had just happened; she just wanted them to be ok.

Just then, one of the guys working in the small bail bond office called us over and said, "Listen, I know you've been here trying to figure something out, but I have been doing this for some time now. His mom just called up here, and she's on her way to post the bail. I would suggest you rest assured knowing that he's being taken care of, but I'm going to ask you to leave so that nothing happens while she's here."

Alexandria totally understood. She was relieved that Landon's mom finally decided to do something. It had been well over 15 hours. As they walked back to Alexandria's car and headed towards the detention center, Alexandria hoped that she could at least see him leave. If she knew that he was no longer in jail, she would be ok. Every other moment Alexandria would just break out in tears.

"I'm really sorry you have to go through this hun," Kimberly said.

"Thanks for being here," she responded.

About two hours later, they saw Landon walk out of the center and get into the car with his mom, dad and one of his friends. He looked ok, but Alexandria wasn't sure. She needed to talk to him. She needed to make sure that everything was ok between us. When they made the decision to be together, her heart told me it would be forever, but this wasn't forever.

***

Later that afternoon, Kimberly took Alexandria home, and she decided to go over to Landon's friend's house. She just sat outside the house thinking if she should muster up the courage to talk to him. She knew Kimberly had done enough, and even though it had been a while, Alexandria decided to call Bonnie.

"Sweetie pie! How are you?" Bonnie exclaimed.

"I'm alright. How've you been?"

She knew that Bonnie may have heard about the situation because we ran in the same circle and the boys still talked. She was still dating Will.

"I'm good. I heard about Landon. Are you ok?"

"Honestly, I'm a mess." As the tears began to flow, Alexandria told Bonnie everything.

"Do you know how he's doing?" Alexandria asked.

"I don't. But if you want, I can try and find something out?"

That's exactly what Alexandria's heart needed. She left Landon's house and went home and waited for Bonnie's call.

It took Bonnie a few hours, but she went over to Alexandria's house to let her know the news.

"He's a bit shaken up, but you know Landon, he's trying to act like he has it all figured out," she said as they sat on the living room couch.

"Did he say anything to you about me?"

"He loves you, Lex. He said that everything happened so fast, but he knows that you weren't trying to lock him up."

Alexandria was relieved to know that Landon wasn't mad at her.

A few days went by, and she hadn't heard from Landon. She tried calling a couple of times, but she had no luck getting in touch with him. She reached out to Bonnie again to see if she knew anything, and she told me that Landon had taken off and no one knew where he was.

"What do you mean he left?"

"He left. I think his mom knows where he is, but he's not here."

I became unsettled, but there was nothing I could do. There was no information that I could obtain. My nerves became really bad, and my emotions were all over the place. My parents were starting to notice my unstable behavior and knew the situation between Landon and I; however, they began to worry about my stability.

One day, my dad called me into the living room.

"Alexandria, your mom and I are concerned about you."

She sat there looking at them because she didn't really have the energy to hide or fight.

"Are you smoking cigarettes?" he finally asked.

"No."

"I was cleaning out your car, and while vacuuming the carpet, I saw a burn hole," he rebutted.

"Your clothes also smell like it," Mrs. Anderson added. I kept looking at them, sticking to the answer she had given.

"Are you still in school? I have been asking for your grades. The agreement was that you could stay here rent free as long as you were finishing up school," Mrs. Anderson followed up.

"Yes." The truth was Alexandria was in school. She was enrolled; she just wasn't attending any of her classes.

"You are keeping your dad up worried at night because you get home late every night. You can stay out, but during the week at least try and come home at a decent hour," her mom said.

Alexandria sat there and listened to them for a while. She wondered if they really thought anything she was saying was true. She looked at them and figured they didn't deserve the headache of dealing with what was actually going on. She wasn't in school. She was drinking more and smoking, and had picked up a second-night job in a bar to help with her habits. She did whatever she could to stay busy, and it was helping keep her mind off the fact that Landon wasn't here.

She made a decision at that moment to leave her parent's house.

"Mom, I know this may seem abrupt, but I'm moving out," she said as she stood in the doorway of Mrs. Anderson's bathroom.

"Where are you going?" Mrs. Anderson asked.

"Into an apartment."

"Alexandria, we aren't asking you to move."

"I know, but I need to do this."

"Is it to be with Landon?" Mrs. Anderson asked concerned.

"Mom, I don't even know where he is. But I just need to move on and grow up. I think moving out will help me."

Alexandria didn't know where she was going, but the next day she got up and packed most of her things and left. She promised her parents that she would still visit and that once she found a place to stay, she would let them know.

Alexandria stayed with Kimberly for the next couple of weeks. It was different, but she felt more in control instead of starring at walls that reminded her of conversations she once had with Landon. She spent almost every night in a bar or a club.

She met new people every day and got drunk until she couldn't remember what was going on. She knew that this wouldn't lead to anything great, but she was gaining more friends, and they were always around. They kept her company during a time when she didn't want to be alone.

They were always high. It got to the point where Alexandria's boss pulled her to the side, one day and inquired, after seeing a box of cigarettes in her car, "Alexandria, do you smoke?"

"No. My friend does, and we ride together a lot."

She looked at Alexandria and said, "You need to get better friends then."

Alexandria didn't think twice about what was said to her that day; she just decided that it would be best if she got another job. She began working with agencies to find another job. She figured she could make more money and not have to worry about keeping up this persona that everyone thought she should have.

***

Two months had gone by, and Alexandria was feeling homesick. She hadn't found an apartment yet, but she knew that she needed help. Though so many people surrounded her, the only person that Alexandria could think about was Landon. She sat in the guest bathroom at Kimberly's, closed the door and began to play music really loud. Alexandria sat there and cried; she wanted to die. If Landon didn't want to be with her, she didn't want to be with anyone else. Alexandria could even stomach to find out he'd moved on to someone else.

She sat there on the floor with tears in her eyes, and all of a sudden, she didn't want to be alive there anymore. She grabbed a razor and cut herself, that night she truly didn't care if she lived or died. Alexandria watched as the blood ran from her wrist onto her hand as she cried. She didn't feel any pain. She didn't want her mom to hurt. In the middle of her breakdown, she didn't want her mom to hurt.

Alexandria picked up her phone and held it in her hand for a while, and she prayed to God again. *God, if you're there, please allow my mom to answer so I can tell her how much she means to me.* She called her mom, and Mrs. Anderson answered.

"Mom."

"What's wrong?" she said concerned. She could tell something was wrong in Alexandria's voice.

"Nothing. I just miss you."

"Are you ok, sweetheart?"

"Yea. I was just sitting here thinking, and I want you to know that you are a great mom. Sometimes children don't tell their parents how much they really mean, but not being there with you and dad has really shown me how much y'all mean to me. I love you."

"I love you too, Alex. You know that as you get older, I will always be here for you. You're my baby."

Alexandria began to cry, but she didn't want her mom to hear the pain that she was in.

Her mom continued, "You be strong for me, ok? I

raised you to be strong."

Alexandria was so confused. All she wanted to say was bye, but that seemed unfair. *If I died a natural death, it wouldn't be as bad; it would be more peaceful to die asleep.* She got off the phone and sat there. She cleaned up her blood, and caught eye of a bottle of NyQuil. She drank the bottle and fought to fall asleep that night. She cried and cried and cried some more.

Alexandria woke up earlier than usual the next morning. She was a little down that she had woke up still in her misery. She felt lost, but different. She knew something would happen that day; she just wasn't sure what.

Kimberly and Alexandria were having dinner and talking about where they were going to go later that night. She hadn't told Kimberly everything she was going through internally. A phone call interrupted their talk. It was an unknown number. She only hoped it was Landon as her heart began to race, she answered, "Hello?"

"Hey, Alex. It's me, Landon."

CHAPTER 19

Landon finally came back to town. They talked for a while, and he told Alexandria that he needed the time away to clear his head and think a lot of things through, but the number one thing that mattered to Alexandria was that he still loved her and wanted to be together. She had so many unanswered questions, but she was just so happy to have him back in her life that she didn't want to dig up old issues.

Landon explained everything that was going on with him when he left and how he didn't want to be like his father. He told Alexandria how the divorce affected him. Landon didn't want to walk out on the woman he loved. She didn't even know that Landon had issues like that. He told her about growing up and how he had a lot of pressure to become a lawyer, and be someone great. But he wasn't passionate about it. Landon also said that he didn't want to be like his cousins in the streets selling drugs, but he wanted to do comedy because he enjoyed making people laugh.

Alexandria gathered that he was trying to figure out life and growing up; and she couldn't fault him for that. She was going through growing pains too, and she still hadn't figured any of it out yet.

*****

They decided that they wanted to work out their relationship and that they would move in together. They finally found an apartment, and within a few weeks, they moved in. It was difficult for Landon because he hadn't found a job since he'd been back. It had become more difficult than before because of his criminal record. Alexandria and Landon spent a few weeks in court trying to work things out. She had even volunteered to testify on Landon's behalf if the case went to trial.

Landon decided to take the guilty plea instead of going through the hassle of a trial. Alexandria helped him pay the probation officer and took him to his anger management classes.

They didn't have much in the apartment when they first moved in, and it took a while for them to really settle in because Landon was going back and forth between his mom's and Alexandria was still moving things from her parent's and Kimberly's, but they decided to do it slowly just as long as they could be together every night.

Landon went along with her new lifestyle of partying, and they spent some of their time with Kimberly and hanging out together. Alexandria found out that Landon picked up a habit of his own while he was away, selling drugs. It was an adjustment, but things were ok between them as they explored life together.

After hearing Landon talk about how difficult it was, dealing with trying not to be like his father, and trying to find a job, she wanted him to understand that she still saw him as a man and he was her man.

Every chance Alexandria got, she would ensure that he was shown in a good light for the family that they were building. Because the apartment was in her name, she was the one with a legal job, and she had to work extra hard to make sure he still felt a part of the process.

When Landon reconnected the weeks before they decided to move in, they talked about a lot of things, but one of the things they talked about the most was having a baby.

In the middle of having sex one night, Landon looked at Alexandria and said. "I want you to have my baby."

"I will."

"No, I want you to have it now."

Alexandria knew that she wasn't ready, but how could she say no?

"Okay," she said looking at him, and moments later

he ejaculated in her.

Alexandria had no idea what she had just done. Then Landon whispered in her ear, "Now, no matter what we will always be together."

It was a difficult couple of weeks ahead because she was nervous about being pregnant. Landon had come to his senses that they probably should have waited until they had their lives together.

A few weeks passed, she got her period. Alexandria was still uncertain so she took a blood test at the Planned Parenthood just to make sure.

Luckily, they were both happy with the outcome. No baby. Landon had moved to Louisiana to live with family while he was away, so he was still back and forth between states, especially since his probation was here.

Alexandria knew that there were some changes that she still wanted to make in her life because she was a long ways off course.

While Landon traveled back and forth, she decided to revisit Dr. Robinson. It was a decision that she'd made on her own this time because she wanted to work out some issues that were still bothering her.

***

"Alexandria! I'm glad you've decided to come back - and this time on your own, that's really big of you. But I have to ask if you want me to be honest with you?"

"Of course."

"You have to want to be honest with yourself."

"Well Doc, I have been."

Alexandria had been very vulnerable with Dr. Robinson and told him everything that happened between leaving for college and where her life was now. He even knew about all her bad habits and how she and Landon decided to move in together.

"Are you happy, Alexandria?"

"What do you mean?"

"Why are you here?"

"Because I need help."

"Do you want me to tell you what to do?"

Yea, that would actually be easy. But she knew that he wouldn't do that. Alexandria just wanted the answer to fix everything that seemed broken. She and Landon were both in a hole. It was this downward spiral stair case, and before she could actually see the light, and now she couldn't see it anymore.

"I know you can't tell me what to do. But can you at least guide me in the right direction? You've always been good at that."

"Alexandria, for years you've come and sat in my office and talked. But you preferred a quick fix instead of a real fix. I've been trying to get you to see that the only way to successfully move forward is to confront your issues – not ignore or bury them."

Alexandria sat there confused. "I don't understand. I've told you everything that has happened."

Dr. Robinson replied, "You've told me what you understand. Have you tried to tell me what you don't?"

"Well, no. But for the most part, I understand everything."

Alexandria didn't understand what Dr. Robinson meant by asking her to try and understand what doesn't make sense. She was reaching out for help, and for some reason, she felt like he didn't want to help her.

"Alex. I want to help you, but you have to trust me. Do you trust me?"

"Of course."

"I want you to go back to your childhood."

She didn't know why she needed to go to her childhood. Alexandria just wanted to grow up normally, graduate from school and marry Landon.

"I don't understand, Doc. What about my childhood is going to help me now?"

"Alex, your relationship with Landon isn't the focus."

Well finally someone was beginning to understand that we were supposed to be together.

"Do you think I should get him to come too?"

Dr. Robinson laughed. "If he really wanted to, I wouldn't mind. But what I mean is, he isn't your problem, neither was any of your past relationships."

Alexandria was so confused. She wasn't sure what Dr. Robinson was trying to say.

"So, I'm the problem?"

"Let's go about this a different way."

"Ok."

"I know two girls, both around the same age. They both grew up in beautiful homes. The house was their safe place and everything that they needed, knew and trusted was in that house. ... Are you following?"

"Yes."

"One day, one of the girls decides to leave the house, just for a while, to play. In the midst of playing, she ends up a long ways from home. All of a sudden, a stranger walks by and pushes her. She falls and gets hurt. People drive by and see her hurt and bleeding, but they don't help. They leave her there."

"Why doesn't she just get up and go home? Are you trying to tell me that I should go home?"

"Listen ...Are you following?"

"Yes, you said one of the girls left her place of safety, and she ends up getting hurt... so, should I have stayed home?"

"Listen Alex. Listen to the story."

"Ok," she said anxiously.

Alexandria was so eager to hear what she should be doing. She just wanted to understand what was wrong with her and how she could fix her relationship.

"So, the second girl that I know, she stayed in the house. She stayed in the place of safety, and the people that she knew, loved and trusted pushed her, and she fell on the floor and got hurt."

"Well, then the home wasn't safe."

"Home is always safe," Dr. Robinson stated.

"Then it wasn't her home," Alexandria shot back.

Dr. Robinson calmly replied, "It was her home."

"Then they were intruders?" Alexandria retorted.

"She knew them; she loved them, she trusted them," Dr. Robinson continued.

"Well then, why did they hurt her? And what does this have to do with me?"

Alexandria was at the edge of her seat. She just wanted the answer.

"Let me finish. So, the second girl locked herself in her room, and because of that, she didn't develop."

"I'm sorry Doc, I'm just trying to understand...did I not develop right?"

"She didn't develop into who she was and instead hid in a dark room. She was afraid of her safe place. She was taunted by this and afraid to come out, even after the people that hurt her left.

By this point, Alexandria didn't know what Dr. Robinson was trying to say.

"Go back. Alex."

She sat there thinking.

"Close your eyes, and try to remember the first memory you had as a child," Dr. Robinson continued.

"Oddly. I remember the day we moved into the house that my parents stay in now. I was in the moving truck in between my uncle and dad, and then I remember setting up our new kitchen with my mom, feeling excited about starting school."

"How old were you?"

Alexandria could remember that day vividly.

"Four."

"Okay, any other memories? Maybe at 5 or 6?"

"No," She lied. She did remember something, but...

"Do you trust me?" Dr. Robinson asked her again.

Alexandria thought she trusted him. She knew she trusted him, but if she told him this memory, what would happen?

"Yea…"

"Just relax and when you're ready, tell me what you remember."

She laid there for a while and thought, *I shouldn't be saying this*. Alexandria fought the memory. *Just say it, Alex!* She told herself.

"I'm 5. I'm in a closet, and my shirt is up, and there is someone on top of me kissing me."

"Who is it?"

She paused. "My cousin."

"Why is he kissing you?"

"I don't know." Alexandria started to cry, "but he has his tongue in my mouth."

"It's okay, Alex."

"Doc?"

"Alex, do you remember this dream?" Dr. Robinson quizzed.

"Doc..." Alexandria replied with her eyes still closed.

"I don't know," she continued.

"Alex, you can do this."

Alexandria was unsure. "How does this help me?"

"You can no longer be taunted by dreams of what happened to you in the past. You've ignored it long enough."

"They don't even bother me anymore." Alexandria replied.

"Alexandria, you can move on past this."

"What do you want me to do, go to my cousin that molested me for ten years and tell him that I don't know how to be in a relationship now? Or should I go to my other cousin that made me go down on him, or my brother's friend that tried to make a move on me? Or my other cousin that had me in his room kissing me. Doc, it was like they all got a memo that went out and said, 'practice on her, she's the stupid one,'" Alexandria frantically said.

"It's ok Alex."

"Landon loves me."

"Landon doesn't know how to love you. You don't even know how to love you."

"Doc, what does this all mean? I don't want to be gross or weird."

"You aren't gross, and you aren't weird. You are broken."

CHAPTER 20

Alexandria woke up out of her sleep from a knock on the door. She looked over to see Landon was still asleep. She quickly go up, wondering whether she should wake him and let him get the door, but before she knew it, she'd already thrown on her robe and opened the bedroom door.

"Where are you going?" Landon whispered because he was awakened out of his sleep from her movement.

Her heart skipped a beat. She didn't want another argument. Alexandria just wanted to stop whoever was at the other side of the door from disturbing the silence.

"Oh, someone's at the door."

"So, what am I here for?" Landon said as he pulled himself out of bed and threw on his shirt. He quickly brushed passed Alexandria as she stood there holding the bedroom door open.

"Who is it?" he shouted from the living room. There was no answer from the other side of the door. He looked through the peephole.

"Who was it?" he asked. "Are you expecting someone?" he looked back and asked her.

"No, I'm not expecting anyone this early. The cable company is supposed to come around lunch though." Alexandria hated the eggshells she walked on. He opened the door, and a menu that was stuck in the crack fell. He bent down to pick it up and quickly closed the door as the cold winter breeze blew in.

Landon walked over and placed the menu on the kitchen counter. He opened the refrigerator and pulled out the gallon of orange juice, opened the bottle and drank from straight from it. It made her light up inside. He knew she hated that. He placed the orange juice back in the refrigerator and walked towards the bedroom. Alexandria was still standing by the doorway.

"Next time, just wake me up," he said as he walked by her to get back in the bed. The 800 square foot apartment all of a sudden seemed pretty small for two people. There was no going back now. She was up, and had some unpacking to do, so she grabbed her phone and headphones and headed into the walk-in closet. Alexandria played her music... got lost in it and quickly finished the closet.

After she had finished, she laid on the floor staring up at the ceiling. She knew she should probably go fix some breakfast, but at that moment all Alexandria wanted to do was be still. She laid on the floor for a while; there was tranquility in that closet. The closet was next to the bathroom, and she heard the toilet seat slam, and quickly got up.

"Hey...are you hungry?" Alexandria asked.

"Yea, but I'm going to pick-up something to eat - you want anything."

"I'm ok. I will make something here."

"You seem busy. You don't even have that much stuff," he laughed.

"Yea, I know. I am just organizing some of your things and mine." Alexandria was pretty annoyed, but she tried not to show it.

"Cool. I'll be back." He quickly threw on some clothes and walked out the door. She went into the bedroom to clean up and make the bed.

***

As Alexandria was finishing up, her phone started to ring.

Ring! Ring! Ring!

"Hey, Bernadine."

"Hey Sweetheart, you don't sound like you're at work."

"I'm at home today. The cable company is stopping by, and I need to be home."

"Oh. Where's that crazy man of yours?"

"He left to go pick-up something to eat. He should be on his way back by now."

"Well, have you eaten?"

"Nope, I was going to find something here."

"Oh, I was calling to see if you wanted to meet up for lunch."

"Today isn't the best day. Especially since Landon is about to head out of town in a few days. We just need to spend some time together before he leaves."

"How are things with you guys anyways?"

"It's ok. Same 'ole, same 'ole." Alexandria kept it brief but still tried to portray the 'work in progress' relationship status.

"Sweetie, I love you. Just let me know when you're free."

"I love you too, and I will."

She knew what everyone wanted to say. She felt it every time she talked to them about Landon. She just believed in him, and she believed that time would heal everything that had happened because she knew that they both wanted to be with each other. She ended the phone call with Bonnie and Landon had made it back. Alexandria was still in the bedroom as she heard him walk towards the closet that was outside the bedroom door. She heard the footsteps coming towards the bedroom.

"Babe?"

"Hey, that was quick!" Alexandria was beginning to feel like she was playing a role on a show, always pretending about the way she truly felt.

"Did you eat?"

"No, I'm heading to the kitchen now."

"I brought you back something anyways."

"Oh, thanks."

Alexandria walked into the kitchen, and waited for him to show her which item he had purchased for her. As Landon followed behind her, he pulled out a to-go container from iHop.

"I got you your usual."

"Perfect. I'm not hungry enough to eat all of this, but it looks delicious."

They sat there eating and flipping through their phones. You could tell that we were both trying really hard. Even in the silence, it was still very distracting. They couldn't watch TV because the cable wasn't working yet, so they sat there eating in silence. Landon looked up from his phone as he was in between bites and said, "Lex, you know I love you right?"

"Yea, of course," Alexandria responded as she looked in his direction.

"It's been a little weird, and I know you feel it too, but I just want you to know that I love you." Landon didn't look at her when he said it, but she understood exactly where he was coming from.

Alexandria reached over and grabbed his hand that was holding the fork and said, "We will get through this." They always got through it, and as long as they were on the same page as far as trying, then Alexandria knew that they would. He took her hand and kissed it. Just then there was a knock on the door. She glanced at the time; it was 11:47AM.

"It must be the cable company," Alexandria said out loud.

Landon got up to check. He opened the door, and greeted the representative who responded by asking for me.

"Alex. The worker is acting like he can't talk to me, so come talk to him."

She sighed. "Why not?" Alexandria got up to from the table and walked to the door.

"Hey. Sir, he lives here."

"Are you Ms. Alexandria Anderson?"

"Yes."

"Ok. It's just that I need the signature of the account holder to make the change."

Landon walked away. Alexandria knew that it annoyed him. She showed the representative in and he got to work. She left him in the living room and walked over to the kitchen.

"Are you ok?" she asked Landon as she cleaned her dishes.

"Yea." He sat there finishing his food. Alexandria placed her plate in the refrigerator, only to be interrupted by the cable representative.

"Ms. Anderson, where would you like the internet router set-up?"

"Oh, right over here." She walked over to show him where the computer was set-up.

***

It took the technician a little over an hour to complete the work. Once he was done, he'd asked her to come over to test everything out.

"I got it," Landon said to them. Alexandria could tell that he'd become frustrated with the fact that the technician kept addressing her.

"No problem sir," the technician said as he began to go through the channel settings with Landon.

Alexandria didn't quite understand all the insecurities that he had ever since the move. They had agreed that since she had the stable job, the apartment would be in her name and utilities would be in his; however, the cable had to be in the name of the lease holder.

"Man, you know if you explain anything to a female, we would have to call you back out here," he said joking with the technician - but Alexandria honestly didn't find it funny. Everything was a power struggle with Landon. Why couldn't he just join them? She didn't understand. She got up from the table and went back into the closet.

Alexandria wanted to just cry because it was becoming too much. She couldn't say what she wanted. She had to guard her every move, and even when she tried to be comforting, it didn't help.

After she heard the front door close, Landon yelled.

"Alex! Alex?"

"I'm in here," she said sitting on the floor in the closet.

"Why are you sitting in here looking stupid?"

"Do you have to go there?" she shot back. "That was embarrassing you know?"

"Why do you act like you have a dick between your legs?"

"I don't understand how I was acting like that. You're very disrespectful."

"I'm not about to do this with you."

"Then don't!" Alexandria knew better than to say what she really felt like saying. She felt if Landon wanted to be treated like a man so bad, then why didn't he just stand up like one. She thought to herself,

I do everything for him. I mean, everything! I let him use my car. I give him money so that when we went out, he looked like he was taking care of it. I even purchase the clothes he wears. What did he want from me? I don't complain. All I did was be available for the cable company to come and hook up the cable that he couldn't grasp had to be directed at me. We aren't even married yet. She was emotional and before she knew it, tears were flowing out of her eyes and her breaths became shorter and faster. She could barely breathe, and felt like she was having a panic attack; something wasn't right.

Alexandria quickly got up. Landon was talking, but she didn't hear anything. The room was spinning, and she needed to get out of the apartment. She tried to get out of the closet, but Landon was standing in the way.

"I need to leave..." Alexandria managed to say.

"I can't breathe, I need air," she said.

Alexandria couldn't stop crying as she stood trying to push pass Landon in the doorway.

"I won't put my hands on you," Landon stated.

She didn't care about that. She just wanted to get out.

"I don't want to fight; I just need some air. Please, Landon!" Alexandria pleaded.

He stood there like a brick wall. She turned around to face the wall, and grabbed her head with both of her hands and fell to the floor on her knees crying. "Landon, please!" was all she said over and over.

"Landon, please...Landon, please...move, Landon, please..." she repeated, rocking back and forth.

Alexandria finally was able to calm herself down and get her breathing under control. She stood up and turned around to see Landon was no longer in the doorway. She quickly grabbed her coat and headed for the front door. She was just about to step outside before she felt him grab her hair and pull her backward.

Alexandria couldn't hear anything. The only thing she felt was numb. She knew she couldn't scream; she didn't say anything. She had fallen to the floor in the foyer. The hardwood floor didn't help with bracing her fall. Alexandria knew the fall had to hurt, but she didn't feel it. Before she could think anything through, Landon's shoe was on top of her head smashing it into the floor. It was something about seeing the bottom of Landon's shoe. In that moment, all she felt was **lower than dirt**, and she bawled like a baby.

Landon quickly unlocked the door and walked out. Alexandria didn't have any fight left in her. She just laid there for what seemed like days. She wondered if he would come back to check on her. She wondered if Landon would come back at all. He always came back. He said that he would always come back, but this time she couldn't chase him.

***

Alexandria laid there until she was about to fall asleep. Just as she was about to drift off, she heard a knock on the door.

Knock! Knock! Knock!

Alexandria could barely move. Her head was throbbing and the vibration on the floor from the knocks made her head hurt even worse. Her face felt tight and her sight appeared to be blurred. Focusing on the limited view she had out window, she could see that day had now become night.

The knocks started again. Alexandria pulled herself off the floor.

Knock! Knock! Knock!

Who can it be? Alexandria thought to herself. When she was finally standing, she unlocked the door and opened it. Standing outside was Bonnie.

"Lex, are you okay?

Everyone has been trying to call you!" Bonnie was frantically crying.

Alexandria literally felt emotionless. There was a tingling feeling in her face. She figured Landon had already told people what happened between them.

"He's gone!" Alexandria assured her, so she wouldn't worry.

"Alex, don't say that. You don't kow that for sure!"

Bonnie walked in and hugged her as she cried.

"It's okay, Bernadine, I'm going to try and be okay with it."

Bonnie let go of Alexandria and wiped the tears that were falling from her face while closing the door.

"You don't look good, Lex. Have a seat."

Bonnie led Alexandria towards the couch, and continued. "He's in bad shape," she said as they sat down. "Everyone's been trying to call you and you're not answering. Did someone get to you before I got here?

Alexandria looked at Bonnie confused. "What are you talking about?" she asked crying. Alexandria's words weren't of concern but irritation. She didn't want to be bothered.

"Alex, sweetheart, Landon was in a serious car accident. He was airlifted to the hospital and he's in critical condition."

Alexandria looked at Bonnie with a blank stare. "Girl! Did you hear me?" Bonnie asked as she stared Alexandria in the face.

In that moment, Alexandria didn't care. She didn't care if Landon had been hurt. She didn't care about the condition he was in. She didn't care about what happened. She was so numb and emotionless, that she didn't even care if he was dead. After all, he did say until death do them part – right?!

CONTACT INFORMATION

Facebook: Martha Kilby

Instagram: @marthakilby

Twitter: @marthakilby

www.marthkilbybooks.com

#HesAGoodGuy #JustNotYours